TOUGH CUSTOMER

Julian hit the stones rolling, shoulders and upper arms absorbing the impact. He lay prone on the cobbles, gun in hand. He shot Red first, drilling him through the middle. McGruff kept coming, his empty gun clicking as he worked the trigger. He loomed large, blotting out the foreground.

Julian shot him. McGruff shuddered, shook it off, kept coming. Julian dropped the gun like a hot iron.

McGruff said, "I'll tear you apart—"

Reaching into his coat, Julian snaked out a four-barreled derringer, and emptied it . . .

JAKE LOGAN

SLOCUM AND THE MOUNTAIN OF GOLD

BERKLEY BOOKS, NEW YORK

SLOCUM AND THE MOUNTAIN OF GOLD

A Berkley Book / published by arrangement with
the author

PRINTING HISTORY
Berkley edition / May 1994

ISBN: 0-425-14231-0

BERKLEY®
Berkley Books are published by
The Berkley Publishing Group, 200 Madison Avenue,
New York, New York 10016.
BERKLEY and the "B" design are trademarks of
Berkley Publishing Corporation.

PRINTED IN THE UNITED STATES OF AMERICA

10 9 8 7 6 5 4 3 2 1

1

The rush was on.

Only one man alive knew the secret as yet: Wade Ramey, twenty-eight, Iowa-born, mean-faced, a killer. A man in a hurry. He ruined his horse racing it down the mountainside, down to the flat where the plains butted up against the foot of the Rocky Mountains. On its last legs, the animal staggered into the town of Blue Meadow, Colorado, with Ramey kicking and cursing it every weary step of the way.

It was an April afternoon. It had rained earlier; blue sky showed through the rifts in the clouds. The road from the south—little more than a trail, really—was a ribbon of brown mud stretching across the fields to a cluster of crude structures that squatted near the base of the eastern slope of the Rockies. Wet ground was matted with coarse short grass, still yellow-brown from winter. Fields were bare of columbines, the blue mountain flowers that had given the town its name. But there was a rich earthy smell in the air that told of the quickening of spring.

Located about midway between Denver in the north and Colorado Springs in the south, Blue Meadow was a supply town that existed off the trade of miners, trappers, and hunters who lived in the mountains. Miners, mostly. The day of the mountain man was thirty years dead. The town lived on, strategically positioned at the start of the rugged Bearclaw Trail that wound through the mountain passes to the high country and the Divide.

Ramey had come down a good part of that steep track fast,

which was why his horse was half-dead as it plodded into town. Its head hung low, close to the earth, ears drooping, eyes filmed over. Heaving sides, foamy with sweat, were cruelly scored with the marks of thornbushes and sharp-edged stones. Red furrows had been gouged into its flanks by Ramey's spurs.

Blue Meadow's main drag was a dirt track running north-south for a hundred yards or so. On either side lay a row of one- and two-story wooden frame buildings. The wood came from timber cut in the hills. Unpainted, it had weathered to a handsome silver-gray color. Roofs were steeply slanted to withstand heavy snows. Windows were few.

Low clouds trailed long snaky arms from their undersides, grazing the white steeple of the town church. The sun peeped in and out, casting a checkerboard pattern of shadow and light across the landscape. Water dripped from the eaves. The recent rain had turned Main Street into a morass. Ramey's horse's hoofs sank deep into the mud with every halting step. Progress was slowed to a crawl.

"Hell, I can walk faster than this!" Ramey said.

He swung down from the saddle, sinking into the muck almost to his boot tops. The horse groaned, breath whuffling from its snout. Blood mixed with saliva where the bit had cut into the sides of its mouth. It shuddered, but was otherwise motionless.

The saddlebags were heavy, both pouches bulging with bulky objects. It was Ramey's turn to groan as he hefted them across his shoulder. His bow legs widened under their weight. His hat became dislodged, but before it could fall he caught it and jammed it tightly onto his head.

Rows of shops fronted both sides of the street. They were bordered by raised wooden plank verandahs that served as walkways. Few people were out-of-doors and they paid scant attention to the arrival of the newcomer. No reason why they should. Ramey wasn't wanted in these parts, not yet. They'd have given him long hard looks if he'd come charging into town all hell-bent-for-leather, like he'd been hours ago at dawn, when he'd first spurred his horse out of the old pros-pector's camp on a mad downhill race. He'd risked his neck a half-dozen times or more during that reckless descent of the Bearclaw Trail. He winced, remembering the crazy chances he'd taken, merely to shave a few extra minutes off his time. The run had used up enough of his horse so that it had slowed to a walk by the time it reached town, thereby attracting little notice from its inhabitants. The rain helped, too. Folks were less likely to stick their noses in other's business if they had to get wet doing it.

The horse stood motionless, panting. It was on the east side of the street, out of the way, so Ramey left it where it was, not even bothering to tie up the reins. It wasn't going anywhere, and if it did, so what? He could buy a dozen horses if he liked; hell, a whole remuda!

The assayer's office was on the other side of the street. Ramey started toward it, crossing at a diagonal. Mud clung to his feet, tugging at his boots as he galumphed along in a clumsy, wide-legged stride.

A merchant's boy was laying planks end to end up ahead, bridging the mired cross street between two blocks of buildings. A slow-moving freight wagon rolled into view at the opposite end of town, entering from the north.

A gliding sunbeam fell on Ramey, pinning him in the middle of the street. He squinted against the sudden dazzling light, scowling. A golden glow outlined him, exposing his hunched, crabbed figure with pitiless clarity. He was soaked to the skin, blackened with trail grime. His clothes would have been shunned by any self-respecting scarecrow. His holstered gun was mud-spattered. Feverish eyes blazed in black-ringed sockets.

A less likely candidate for holder of the key to untold wealth would have been hard to find. But it was true. Ramey was sole possessor of the secret of a bonanza of hidden riches. He was within sight of the assay office where he would establish legal claim to the ownership of that fortune.

And then he met John Slocum.

The hole in the clouds closed; the sunbeam faded, vanished. Before Ramey could resume his trek, a voice rang out:

"Ramey! Wade Ramey!"

Ramey had heard enough men being called out before to

know that now his turn had come. He glanced at his gun. He didn't reach for it or even move. He knew without seeing that the caller had the drop on him, too. That's how he, Ramey, would have handled it.

At first, he didn't even see his antagonist. A boot heel scraping on a floorboard caught his attention. The sound was made by a man with a rifle who stood on the east side of the street, on the walkway, to the right and slightly behind Ramey, who had to turn to see him.

It was hard to make him out. Gray gloom massed under the overhanging balcony beneath which the stranger stood. The ground floor of the building was occupied by a store, the upper level held living quarters. The stranger was to the right of the street door, his back to the wall. His clothes were brown and gray, neutral colors that tended to blend into the background. The bore of the Winchester he held in both hands leveled at Ramey was a coin-sized disc, blacker than black.

A big man, he was long, lean, rawboned. A holstered Colt hung low off his right hip and a fifteen-inch bowie knife lay sheathed on his left side. He was almost as ragged and filthy as Ramey. He looked like a trail herder, a top hand who had been doing some hard riding.

He's a top hand, all right, Ramey said to himself. A top *gun* hand.

"Ramey," the stranger said. He spoke less loudly, now that he had the other's attention.

Ramey, bluffing, screwed up his face in an expression of monumental incomprehension, shrugged, and made as if to go about his business.

"Hey," the stranger said.

Ramey froze. His horse's ears pricked up with interest. Ramey tried another tack. "Point that thing somewhere else, mister," he said.

The stranger didn't bother to respond. Pale eyes glittered in his weathered face.

Ramey frowned, puzzled and mad, fighting to keep the mad down.

"I don't know you," he said.

"I know you, Ramey," the other said.

"I don't know who you think I am, but whoever it is, I ain't him. You got the wrong man, mister."

"You answered to the name quick enough."

Ramey shook his head. "I was just looking 'round to see who was hollering," he said.

"Funny, you look just like the picture on a wanted circular I've got in my pocket. I'd show it to you, but my hands are kind of busy right now," said the stranger.

The rifle muzzle held rock-steady on a line even with Ramey's middle.

Ramey looked longingly at his gun, hands shaking with eagerness to make a grab for it. He balled them into fists instead.

He said, "I ain't wanted for nothing, mister."

"Not for nothing, Ramey. For five hundred dollars."

Ramey laughed, a harsh ragged caw.

"Five hundred dollars—?! Ain't nobody'd post so much as five hundred pennies on my poor old hide!"

"I wouldn't, but your friends back in Brushcut did," the stranger said.

"B-Brushcut?"

"Brushcut, Kansas, Ramey. You know."

Ramey tried a show of guileless innocence. He said, "I swear on my mother's life that I've never so much as set foot in Kansas!"

"Save your breath for the hangman's rope. The old gal lived."

"I—huh?"

"Old Mrs. Hurley. She lived."

That burned Ramey like a hot iron. "Damn her! I put an extra slug into the old witch, just to make sure, and she still don't die—"

He was furious.

"Tough old gal," the stranger said.

Ramey looked around. The merchant's boy had stopped what he was doing to watch the show. Idlers in front of the feed store turned to see what it was all about. Unalarmed, they were as yet merely curious.

At the far end of the street, the freight wagon lumbered on, seeming little closer than it had been when it first appeared minutes ago.

Ramey said, "Who're you?"

"Slocum," the other said.

"You don't look like no lawman."

"You don't look like you're worth five hundred dollars, but you are."

"Somebody's been pulling your leg, Slocum. There ain't five hundred dollars to be found in all that shithole town."

"Town didn't post the bounty, Ramey. Railroad did."

"Bullshit. What happened—and I ain't saying anything did happen, mind you—but even if it did, it ain't no skin off the railroad's ass, no sir!"

Ramey feared not the law but the railroad. The Iron Horse was a power in the West. Lawmen had jurisdictions but the railroad was everywhere. Bad medicine to cross. He steered clear of anything that might run afoul of the roads, even to the extent of not committing crimes anywhere along a right of way.

"Colonel Appleton swung the deal. He was mighty close to those Hurleys. Like one of the family, almost," Slocum said.

Ramey grunted. Appleton, a railroad business agent and promoter, was one of the biggest men in West Kansas.

That was worrisome and Ramey didn't like to be worried. Resentment made him burn. Burning was better than worry, it bucked up his nerve. The railroad wasn't almighty God and Colonel Appleton wasn't His avenging angel. A railroad was people, and they could be bought off, same as everybody else, as long as you had the gold. Ramey had the gold, by God!

He said, "You fixing to kill me, Slocum?"

"That depends."

"On what?"

"On you. I'm taking you in. If you want to make a play, do it," Slocum said.

"You gonna give me a chance at a fair draw?"

Slocum smiled, white teeth flashing in a bronzed face.

"You son of a bitch," Ramey said.

"If you want to live, unbuckle your gunbelt. Slowly."

"You like hunting men for blood money, Slocum?"

"Sometimes. Like now."

Ramey sneered. "Five hundred dollars . . . how'd you like to make ten times that amount?"

"Five thousand dollars . . . just for letting you go, eh?"

"That's right. Five thousand dollars. What do you think of that, Mr. Bounty Hunter?"

"Why not make it fifty thousand? Or five hundred thousand, as long as you're telling a tall one?"

"Don't believe me, huh? About having the money, I mean."

"You couldn't scrape up five cents, from the looks of you."

"Wrong," Ramey said.

His confidence was returning. He felt on surer ground now. For one thing, he wasn't bluffing. He could do what he said, pay what he promised.

"This is your lucky day, cowboy," he began.

"I'll say it is. I just made myself five hundred dollars. Speaking of which, you've still got that gunbelt on," Slocum said.

A prompting gesture with the business end of the rifle lent weight to his words.

"You won't kill me," Ramey said. "You can't."

"No?"

"Not without throwing away five thousand dollars."

"You can't lose what never was."

"You'll lose five thousand if you don't hear me out."

"I'm losing patience waiting for you to drop that gunbelt," Slocum said.

Ramey held up his hands palms outward.

"All right, all right. Don't shoot. I'm doing it," he said.

His hands drifted down to his waist, battening on the gunbelt's buckle and strap, undoing them slowly, deliberately.

He said, "Now, just ease off of that trigger long enough to let me make you a rich man, Slocum—"

"Talk fast, it's a long ride back to Kansas."

Fear, greed, and rage warred in Ramey, choking him. Losing control, he spoke without thinking.

"There's a small fortune in these saddlebags and that's not even the smallest part of the riches waiting to be taken and you, all you can think of is your stinking blood money, you damned piker!"

At that moment the doors of a nearby saloon crashed open as an individual was summarily ejected from the premises. He was thrown out the door so hard that he sailed across the verandah without touching it as he landed in the street with a belly flop, facedown, his fall cushioned by the muck.

The barkeep stalked outside, a big brute with a prizefighter's physique. Thin hair, parted in the middle, was slicked back against his skull. A thin mustache, neatly clipped. A stiff-collared striped shirt, sleeves rolled up over the elbows of brawny forearms.

Unaware of the tense drama taking place a stone's throw away from him, the barkeep strode out to the edge of the walkway, jamming big fists on his hips as he glared down at the man sprawled prone in the mud.

"Next time you'll get worse, you lousy drunk!" he said.

When the drunk first came catapulting out of the saloon, Slocum looked away from Ramey toward the site of the disturbance.

Ramey grabbed his gun. Before it could clear the leather, Slocum fired.

Flames ringed the rifle bore. A loud report boomed.

The slug took Ramey a few inches above the navel. He pitched backward. The fall popped open the top of his saddle-bag pouches, spilling a mass of fist-sized rocks into the mud.

Ramey lay faceup on his back with a hole in his middle. His eyes were open but unseeing.

The puff of gunsmoke was scrambled by stiff breezes, so that only a thin gray wisp clung writhing to the rifle muzzle.

The ejected brass of the round jingled on the wooden sidewalk like a spun coin.

The barkeep had been self-satisfiedly brushing his palms together when the shot sounded. He stood frozen in that position. The drunk raised himself on his elbows, prying his upper body free of the muck covering him from head to toe. He seemed made of mud. He stared, unable to focus his eyes. He saw three riflemen and three corpses and three horizon lines, all of which were rising and falling like a stormy sea.

The merchant's boy goggled. The idlers crouched, ready to run for cover. The wagoneer reined in his team, standing up to better see what was happening at the south end of town.

Wind-whipped clouds surged east across the sky, a fast-running gray torrent.

The spinning brass cartridge fell through the slit between two planks, vanishing.

Ramey's horse snorted.

The barkeep said, "My God, he's killed him!"

"Killed? Gawd!" cried the drunk.

He threw himself face-flat in the mud.

The idlers scattered. The wagoneer whipped his team into action. Hoofs and wheels churned up dirt as the wagon slowed around a corner and disappeared down a cross street.

Slocum had brought the rifle in case Ramey had friends. He kept his back to the wall for the same reason. Lines of tension etched his face, showing through the grime.

He swung the weapon to cover the barkeep, who threw up his hands in horror.

Slocum said, "Any objections?"

"Hell, no! This ain't nothing to me," the barkeep said.

"That's right," Slocum said. "Go tend your bottles."

The barkeep nodded, not moving.

Slocum jerked his head in the direction of the saloon. "Git."

Bobbing his head gratefully, the barkeep lunged through the swinging doors, inside.

Slocum looked around, eyes narrowed, searching. No immediate threat presented itself. Creases on his forehead and at the corners of his eyes eased, smoothing out. Some, but not all, of the tightness left his face. The rifle barrel angled toward the ground, but could be leveled for action in an eye blink.

The merchant's boy stood in place, gawking, openmouthed. He said, "Gee, mister, what for did you kill that fellow?"

For five hundred dollars, thought Slocum.

"He was reaching," Slocum said.

"Oh."

The youngster nodded, satisfied with the explanation.

"C'mere, kid," Slocum said.

"Me?"

"You."

The towheaded, freckle-faced kid, about ten or eleven years old, came toward Slocum, scuffling his shoes against the planked walkway. Detouring to its edge, he hooked his hand around a support post and leaned far out over the street, staring down at Ramey.

"Whew! That sure is a big hole in him," he said.

"He put one like it in a boy about your age," Slocum said.

"Why?"

"Never mind about that. He was a bad hombre, that's all you need to know."

"If you say so."

"I do say so."

"He an outlaw, mister?"

"He was."

"You an outlaw?"

"Do I look like an outlaw, boy?"

The youngster nodded solemnly. "Yep," he said.

"Well, I'm not," Slocum snapped.

"If you say so."

"Who's the law in this town, kid?"

"Sheriff Larch."

"Honest man?"

"Sure," the boy said, surprised at the question.

"That is, I reckon he's honest," he added, after a pause.

Slocum reached into an inside pocket of his coat, fishing out a long oilskin envelope bulging with folded papers. Unfolded, they were revealed as documents, blazoned with official letterheads, stamps, and seals. Slocum thrust the sheaf of papers at the boy.

"Here, give these to the sheriff. They might save some shooting," he said.

The boy remained inert.

"Go on, take them," Slocum said.

The boy took them and started reading the uppermost paper, moving his lips as he did so.

Slocum said, "You can read?"

"Some," the boy admitted.

"Can the sheriff?"

The boy shrugged.

"If not, make sure that somebody reads them to him before he comes over here or there's liable to be a fuss," Slocum said.

He flipped a silver dollar at the boy, who adroitly caught it one-handed.

"For your trouble," Slocum said.

"Thanks, mister!"

The coin was swallowed up in the depths of the boy's trouser pocket.

"Don't dawdle," Slocum said.

"No, sir."

The lad couldn't leave without taking one last lingering look at the corpse.

Slocum said, "Scat!"

The boy took off running.

Sheriff Asa Larch made his way south along the west side of the street, moving with well-considered deliberateness. No sense in running headlong into a bullet.

He was burly, barrel-chested, bullish. A big gut slopped over the top of his gunbelt, jiggling as he bore down on the trouble site. He gnawed the ends of his mustache, which looked like a piece of dirty, greasy rope that had been stuck onto his upper lip. Pinned to his vest over his heart was a lead-colored badge, dull, tarnished. He kept it that way on the theory that it made a less attractive target than a bright, shiny badge. Larch missed few opportunities to maximize his chances.

A half-dozen paces behind, and moving up fast, was Buck, Larch's deputy. Buck was fifty pounds lighter and twenty years younger than his boss. He'd never get fat on a Blue Meadow deputy's salary. He planned to get ahead. His badge, well polished, shone like a newly minted coin. His face was pockmarked where his brown-black beard didn't cover it. Black button eyes. He toted a shotgun in addition to his sidearm.

He soon overtook Larch, who continued at an unhurried

pace. If Buck got a few steps out in front, that was fine with Larch.

A citizen crouching for cover behind a rain barrel stuck his head out to one side as the lawmen neared.

"He's got a rifle!" he said.

Buck hesitated in his stride, then squared his shoulders and kept in step, though less swiftly. Larch smirked.

Buck paused at the corner, waiting for him.

"What's he doing?" Larch said.

"Smoking a cigar, looks like," Buck said.

"There's a cold-blooded killer for you!"

Larch squinted south. "I see two bodies, Buck."

"Yah."

"But I only heard one shot."

"Huh!"

Buck pushed back his hat and scratched his forehead. "That's a puzzler," he said.

"Reckon we'd better go solve it, Deputy."

"Right."

Neither one moved. Up ran the boy, arms pumping, legs flashing, calling the sheriff's name.

Larch said, "Look at that fool kid."

"That's Clyde, the merchant's boy," Buck said.

"Running around like a chicken with his head cut off."

Clyde skidded to a half in front of the lawmen. He was red-faced, breathless. Holding the sheaf of papers at arm's length, he waved them at the duo, indicating that they should take them.

"Ain't you got enough sense not to run around in the open at a time like this, you crazy kid? You want to get your damn fool head blown off?" said Larch.

Clyde's paper waving grew more frantic.

Buck said, "What you got there, boy?"

Clyde managed to gasp out a few words between panting breaths.

"From *him*—back there—told me to give these to the sheriff," he said.

"Him? Him who, the killer?" Buck said.

The boy nodded so hard that his eyes rolled.

"Let me see that," Buck said. He took the papers. "What we got here?" he said.

"Give me those," Larch said. He grabbed the bundle out of Buck's hand.

"For the sheriff, the boy said. That's me, or at least it was, the last time I looked," Larch said.

Buck forbore to reply. He was used to Larch's ways.

Unfolding them, smoothing out the creases, Larch held the papers in both hands, studying them from various angles for a moment before thrusting them back at Buck.

"I can't make head nor tail out of them chicken scratches without my reading glasses. Here, you take a gander at 'em, Buck."

"Okay, Asa."

Buck riffled through the papers. Larch spoke to the boy.

"Get off the street, and I mean pronto," he said.

"Aw, I ain't scared," Clyde said.

"Don't sass me, boy, or I'll give you the back of my hand!"

He would have, too, but Clyde was out of reach and he couldn't smack him without exposing more of himself than he cared to. The killer had a rifle . . .

"I didn't mean nothing, Sheriff. But the stranger won't shoot you," Clyde said.

"That's for sure," said Larch.

"He's a lawman!"

"That killer? He's a cold and calculating desperado, boy, and make no mistake."

"I'm not so sure of that, Asa," Buck said, unhappy. "According to what I see here, the kid's right."

"The hell you say."

Buck flourished the topmost sheet of paper.

"This is written on the letterhead of the U.S. Marshal's office in Brushcut, Kansas. It names the bearer as a duly appointed officer charged with the capture of a wanted fugitive, one Wade Ramey, by any means necessary—*dead or alive*," he said.

"A bounty hunter," Larch said.

"That's the gist of it."

"How is he called—the bounty man?"

"Slocum."

"What's the rest of it?"

Buck studied the text.

"It just says 'Slocum.' That's all," he said.

"No first name?"

"Maybe that is his first name."

"I don't like it," Larch said.

"This piece of paper is real, Asa. It's stamped and notarized and all," Buck said.

Larch glowered. "Why'd he have to pick my town?"

There was no answer to that one.

"What's he doing, Buck?"

"Still smoking."

"Arrogant bastard."

"Looks like he's waiting on us, Asa."

"Let him wait. What else is in them papers?"

Buck shuffled the sheets.

"This one's from some high muckety-muck in the Kansas Pacific," he said.

Skimming the text, he read aloud:

"'All employees of the line are hereby directed to extend every cooperation to Mr. Slocum . . .'"

"Huh! Wonder what the railroad wants in this? An express mail robbery, most likely. The line would hound the robbers to the ends of the earth," Larch said.

"Maybe this fellow Ramey was mixed up in something like that."

"Maybe so, Buck, maybe so. Still, Kansas is a long way off. We've got laws here in Colorado to protect folks against backshooting bounty killers."

"We don't know that he did shoot him in the back, Asa."

"He did, mark my word on it. All them bounty men are backshooters. Scavengers, the whole dirty murdering lot."

"I didn't know you felt that strongly about it."

"Well, I do, I do. The people of this town got a right to be protected against railroad hired guns shooting down folks in the middle of Main Street in broad daylight! Somebody's going to have to pay a pretty penny to square it. Maybe the stranger, maybe the KP. Maybe both," Larch said.

Winking broadly, Larch hitched up his gunbelt, snugging it under his belly roll.

He said, "Man, you sure got a long face on you, Buck. Cheer up! There won't be no shooting. The bounty man don't want trouble, he just wants his money. And if spreading a little some of it around the Blue Meadow sheriff's office speeds him on his way, why, he'll pay. He won't like it, but he'll pay, long as we don't take too big a bite—why you shaking your head no?"

Buck held up a third document.

"This one's got the letterhead of the Denver and Rio Grande. It's just like the KP letter, except that it's not just made out to railroad employees. It's more general. It includes 'all peace officers and law enforcement agencies . . . requested to furnish all possible assistance' to . . . Slocum," he said.

"And it's signed by Fulbright himself!" he added.

"Fulbright! Why, he's one of Palmer's top men! Let me see that," Larch said.

He grabbed the letter.

"I ain't much on reading, but I know the D&RG sign when I see it. This's genuine, all right," Larch conceded.

"What do we do now?" Buck said.

"We go say how-do to Mr. Slocum, that son of a bitch. Me, I ain't so big but that I can't use some goodwill from the D&RG, damn them."

"We sure don't want their bad will."

"Hell, no!" Larch said, shuddering.

There wasn't a set of tracks within sight of Blue Meadow, but the lines weren't too far distant. Few spots in this part of the state were beyond the reach of the ubiquitous iron rails. Not long ago, only a few years back, the rival Denver and Rio Grande and Santa Fe lines had gone to war over their competing claims to the same right-of-way. Both companies brought in private armies of ex-soldiers and gunslingers who battled it out from the prairies to the mountain passes in some of the fiercest fighting seen in the region since the War Between the States. The dispute had been settled by the signing of a new contract between the claimants, but memories of the clash were still raw among Coloradans.

Warily, and without enthusiasm, Larch and Buck went down the street, keeping to the wooden sidewalks to avoid being enmired in the muck of the main thoroughfare.

The absence of renewed gunfire emboldened more of the citizenry to investigate the fatal event. Pale oval faces appeared at windows, peeking through parted curtains. Heads were thrust out of doors, craning out from beyond the cover of door frames and blind corners.

Coming to the last cross street above the place where the bodies lay, Larch and Buck stepped down into the mud and trudged down Main Street. The muck made sucking sounds when they lifted their boots out of it. They had to step lively to avoid the many piles of horse apples studding the road.

They plodded to a halt near the northernmost body stretched in the street. It lay facedown.

Larch said, "Who's that?"

"It's Highgrade," Buck said.

"Highgrade! What'd he want to go and shoot him for? If that ain't the meanest thing I ever seen, gunning down a harmless old drunk who never hurt nobody—!"

Highgrade lifted his face out of the mud. "I ain't killed, Sheriff."

"You hit bad, Highgrade?"

"I ain't hit at all, so far as I can tell, Buck."

"Then what the hell you doing lying in the middle of the street?" Larch said.

"Seemed like the safest place to be, once the shooting started."

"Bah!"

Raw whiskey fumes and less pleasant smells poured off Highgrade, so strong that they brought tears to Buck's eyes.

"Gad!" he said.

He stepped back, fanning the air in front of his face as if to clear it.

"Lucky thing Highgrade wasn't hit. With all the redeye he's got in him, he'd have blown up and taken half the town with him," Buck said.

"Don't be unkind, Buck. There's enough meanness in the world as it is. Like Fitz," Highgrade said.

"Fitz" Fitzhugh was the barkeep who had tossed Highgrade into the street.

Buck said, "What about Fitz?"

"He threw me out on my ear, like I didn't have a penny to my name. Which I don't, but that's no reason for him to get tough. I could have got hurt."

"Maybe he didn't like you drinking for free, Highgrade."

"Everybody knows I'm good for the money. I've just had a little run of bad luck lately."

"Sure. Like for about twenty years or so."

"C'mon, Buck. We're wasting our time on this sot," Larch said. "Too bad Fitz didn't break his damn fool neck."

"Is that nice, Sheriff?"

"Shut up, Highgrade."

"Yes, sir."

A man rushed out of the mercantile store. Fussy, pinch-faced, graying, he wore a shopkeeper's white bib apron over his clothes.

"Clyde! Clyde! Have you seen my boy, Sheriff?" he said.

"Finally got around to missing him, did you?" Larch said.

"Clyde's fine, George," Buck said.

"Thank God!"

George surveyed the scene.

He said, "Not again! I thought we were through with the killing! Won't this violence ever stop?"

"Not so long as man endures," Highgrade said.

"You just keep your trap shut, Highgrade! Nobody's talking to you!"

"Ah, would that it were so."

"That fancy talk doesn't fool anyone! You're a disgrace! Wallowing around in the street like a hog in a mud hole! If you had an ounce of self-respect, you'd pick yourself up and stand on your own two feet like a man. That is, if you're not too drunk to."

"I figure I'm safer here if there's more shooting."

"More—shooting?" George said.

He paused, paling, then started backing away toward the

shop door, casting nervous sidelong glances at Slocum, the sheriff, and his deputy.

Safely across the threshold, George shook his fist at Highgrade.

"You ought to be run out of town on a rail!" he said.

"Sure, and you'd sell them the rail at a nice tidy profit for youself, eh, George? Nobody's going to run off old Highgrade. Without me, who'd you all have to feel superior to?" Highgrade said.

"There ain't gonna be no more shooting, I can tell you that," Larch said.

He was speaking not to George but to Slocum.

Slocum puffed away on a stinking cigar. It looked like it had been cut from the same piece of greasy, dirty rope as the sheriff's mustache. A gray smoke ghost writhed above his head, torn by the wind but renewed with each fresh puff.

He stood leaning with his back against a wall, one leg bent at the knee. He held the rifle in his right hand, pointing downward.

Larch said, "You Slocum?"

"Yah."

"Why'd you up and kill this man in my town, Slocum?"

"It's where I found him."

"You should have come to me first. When a fellow's going to be shot down like a dog on Main Street, I like to know about it in advance. A little matter of professional courtesy, if nothing else. 'Course, I'm only the sheriff of this here town, so maybe you could say I'm being a mite oversensitive, but that's how I feel about it."

"Sorry, Sheriff."

"It's easier on the nerves, too. My nerves, that is. I don't like surprises. You could of got shot yourself, being mistook for a common outlaw," Larch said.

He seemed to relish the prospect.

"Sorry Sheriff, but there wasn't time. It all happened kind of fast. I was just riding into town for supplies when I spotted the man I've been trailing. I braced him as soon as he got down from his horse. He reached, and that was that," Slocum said.

"Lucky break for you," Buck said.

"Wasn't it?" Slocum said.

"It wasn't for him," Larch said.

Slocum neglected to mention his other reason for keeping his plans to himself: the fact that all too often the local law was in league with the lawless.

The sheriff jerked a thumb in the direction of the corpse. "That Ramey?" he said.

"Uh-huh," Slocum said.

"What'd he do to deserve killing?"

"Rape and murder. And plenty more besides, but that's what he's wanted for back in Kansas. Some folks named Hurley were riding their wagon into town when they crossed trails with him. A grandmother, her eighteen-year-old granddaughter and ten-year-old grandson. He came across their wagon on a lonely stretch of road. It started as a holdup. The old woman did something he didn't like so he shot her. The boy started running and was shot in the back. Ramey had his way with the girl and shot her, too. The old gal came around while he was robbing the bodies, so he shot her again. He rode off, but the old gal wasn't dead. She lived to tell the tale and point the finger at Ramey. He was a well-known troublemaker in those parts and it was easy to identify him from her description," Slocum said.

"Them Hurleys kin to you?"

"No."

"In it for the reward money, eh?"

"No, I just like to shoot people. The money's the icing on the cake."

Buck said, "Where does the railroad come in, Slocum?"

"Colonel Appleton's assistant was engaged to marry the girl. The colonel was plain and determined to see her killer brought to justice, and he's a mighty big man in the KP."

"Big man," Larch said. "He wouldn't have done the same for my daughter, I'll bet."

"You don't have a daughter," Buck said.

"I know that, you blamed idiot! That was just a manner of speaking. What I meant was, if I had a daughter, this here Appleton wouldn't care two cents if she lived or died. Or your daughter. And don't go telling me that you ain't got a daughter because I know that, too. The point is, the railroad takes care of its own, and to hell with everybody else!"

"Say what you like about Appleton, Sheriff. He's no kin of mine," Slocum said.

Buck squatted down beside the body.

Larch said, "What you doing, Buck?"

"He must have been up in the hills prospecting. His saddlebags are full of rock samples," Buck said.

"I'd say the bounty man struck it rich instead."

"I'm not so sure," Buck said.

He held a chunk of rock in his hands, turning it over, peering at it. The size of a pair of fists held together, it was surprisingly heavy for its size. Scrutinizing it from various angles, Buck was thoughtful, intent. He rubbed it with his sleeve, clearing some of the dirt off it.

The shifting checkerboard of shadow and light caused by the sun shining through streaming clouds once more rearranged itself, laying a tilted square of light on the street. As it fell on Buck and the dead man, the sunbeam struck fire as it touched the rock in the deputy's hands. Gold veins streaking the ore leapt into prominence, blazing forth as if molten.

A golden beacon, it shone more brightly still by contrast to the cool blue-gray shadows swathing its immediate surroundings.

Buck's eyes were dazzled. Slocum's eyes narrowed. Highgrade grunted, as if struck in the stomach.

"Great God A'mighty," Larch said.

He spoke soft-voiced, but in the sudden hush that had fallen, his words sounded gratingly loud to his own ears.

No one else even heard him, so entranced were they all by the golden vision.

The streaming clouds re-formed, blotting out the sunbeam, and the vision passed. Golden afterimages persisted, hanging in the air for a half-dozen heartbeats before vanishing.

Awestruck wonder marked the faces of those who had seen the golden glory.

The Annunciation.

Slocum's face was a mask of fury. He had cheated himself out of a bonanza of gold by shooting first and asking later.

He felt like giving himself a good swift kick. Then he saw the humor in the situation and forced a sour grin.

"That's one on me," he said.

His voice, a harsh croak, broke the spell. Wonderment was replaced by greed and naked self-interest among the beholders.

Buck held the ore fragment like it was a holy relic. The rock was marbled with gold veins, shooting through it like the traceries on the underside of a leaf. Denied the burnishing of the sun, the threads were a dull, metallic reddish-gold web laced through milky gray-white quartz.

Larch said, "What you got there, Buck?"

He tried to sound casual but was breathless and rasping. Squelching through the mud over to the body, he stood so his boots toed Ramey's saddlebags.

Buck rose off his haunches, taking the strain off his knees and thighs. He cradled the ore.

Larch grabbed it away from him.

"Let me see that," he said.

The deputy shot him a glance of pure hate, but Larch was too engrossed in the rock specimen to notice, or care if he had noticed.

"Got some color in it," he said at last.

Buck nodded, tight-lipped.

"'Course, that don't mean nothing by itself. Many a man's had his heart broke by fool's gold," he said.

While thus musing aloud, he turned the rock over in his hands, eyeing it keenly.

"Good color, though," he said.

Taking out his pocketknife, he unfolded a blade and scratched the tip against one of the metallic veins, scraping off minute little shavings.

"Soft," he said.

Highgrade managed to get up on his hands and knees and watched, crouching. The barkeep stepped out of the saloon, followed by a few inquisitive patrons. They were as drunk as Highgrade but had the money to pay for it, ensuring their welcome until the cash ran out. There were three of them, two ranch hands in town to pick up supplies and a fancily dressed drummer hawking drill bits. The hired men stood with an arm around each other's shoulders, holding each other up. The drummer went to lean against an upright support post, misjudged, and bumped his head against it. A loud hard knock sounded, but the brim of his derby absorbed most of the blow. The drummer blinked owlishly. Scandalized, a pair of middle-aged women watching through the front window of the general store tsk-tsked and cluck-clucked.

Up and down both sides of the street, people were emerging from indoors, filtering outside in small groups, hesitantly but inexorably drawn to the scene of the killing. Not the dead man but his bright-glinting ore was the bull's-eye toward which they all arrowed. This was Colorado, where millions of dollars' worth of gold and silver had been torn from the earth and untold millions more lay hidden, waiting to be struck.

Slocum stood at the edge of the sidewalk, ignored in the commotion.

It was Larch's turn to glare at his subordinate, as Buck reached into the saddlebag and hauled another chunk into view. Brushing aside dirt, he revealed gold-streaked facets of smoky quartz.

"Do you suppose it's real?" he said.

"Naw," Larch said.

His denial convinced no one, not even himself.

A crowd, three deep and steadily growing, ringed the lawmen.

"All right, break it up. Move along, there. This ain't none of your business anyhow, so git," Larch said.

"Gold is everybody's business," George said.

The shopkeeper stood at the fore of the crowd, all of whom signaled their vigorous agreement with his statement.

Larch stifled the impulse to give George the back of his hand. He said, "Who says it's gold?"

"Well, isn't it?" George said.

The crowd pressed closer. Larch picked up the saddlebags, grunting from the effort. They were heavy with ore.

"What's in there?" somebody said.

"Evidence," said Larch.

Somebody else said, "Get Bissell! He'll know!"

Others took up the cry. Bissell was the town assayer.

The mood hung fire between elation and despair as the crowd waited for Bissell to arrive and deliver the verdict.

Slocum said, "Hey, Sheriff."

"What do you want?"

"I need my paperwork back, now that you've seen it."

Larch handed over the wadded bundle.

"Take 'em and be damned!" he said.

"Thanks," Slocum said.

Smoothing out the creases, he carefully refolded the three documents, put them into the oilskin envelope, and pocketed it.

"Hell of a thing, when you can't kill a man unless you've got an official permit to do so. Looks like civilization has come to the West," Slocum said.

Someone safely cloaked in the anonymity of the crowd spoke up: "What do you know about all this, stranger?"

"Not a damn thing. You'll have to ask him," Slocum said, meaning Ramey.

"Here's Bissell!" another cried.

The ranks parted to make way for the assayer, a medium-sized man with thinning fair hair and small, neat hands and feet. He was hatless, coatless, and in a hurry. Stepping to the front, he took in the scene with a glance that included the corpse, the lawmen, and the rock samples that were the center of attention.

"Take a look at this, Russ," Larch said.

He handed the rock to the assayer. He stood beside Bissell, ready to put the arm on him in the unlikely event that the latter should be so overcome with greed as to try to run away with the stone.

Bissell's first good look at the sample narrowed his eyes with hard interest. A few seconds more of shrewd professional appraisal caused his eyebrows to lift and his eyes to widen. A spasm flickered across his face, like a lake surface ruffled by a breeze. He masked his reaction with a poker face, but it had already been seen.

"Ah," someone said.

It was not a sigh but rather a half-stifled gasp of excitement. An electric thrill went through the assembled.

Larch said, "Well?"

"Interesting," Bissell said. "Who found it?"

"Him," Larch said, pointing at Ramey.

"Too bad."

"Quit stalling, Russ. It is genuine or not?"

"Uh, well, it's hard to say on such short notice. It, uh, looks promising, but I'll have to run a series of tests on it before I can say for sure, one way or the other."

"But it looks promising, you say?"

"Well . . . yes."

A fever had come over the crowd, leaving its members flush-flaced and glittering-eyed. Gold fever.

"What kind of double-talk is that?" Highgrade said.

Having managed to rise up on two feet, he lurched into the open oval ringed by the crowd. Reeling as if buffeted by gale-force winds, he remained upright thanks to some internal stabilizing gyroscope. Mud-fronted from head to toe, he knuckled the stuff away from his eyes to see better.

"Pass that rock over here, brother," he said.

"You're drunk!" Bissell said.

"Drunk or sober, I know my gold. Let's have a looksee . . . "

Hoots and jeers welled up around Highgrade. The mud helped, because nobody wanted to soil themselves by laying hands on him to drag him away.

Larch reached for his gun, intending to club the drunk with it. His hand closed around the butt, but he hesitated to draw it, suddenly conscious of Slocum hovering somewhere around the periphery. It might not be healthy to draw with the bounty hunter in the vicinity. Slocum might misunderstand and think that he was the target . . . and he had already killed once today.

While Larch paused, barkeep Fitzhugh made himself heard.

"He's a drunk, by God, but I've never known Highgrade to be wrong about gold! Give him a look," he said.

With a volatility characteristic of crowds, this one began clamoring for Highgrade to be allowed to examine the rock. Nothing would do but that he be allowed to pass judgment.

Bissell handed over the rock with no less reluctance than Larch had shown earlier when handing it over to him.

Highgrade peered at the ore through rheumy, bloodshot eyes

that were not without a hint of canniness flickering in their depths.

"I sure could use a drink," he began.

"Don't push your luck, Highgrade."

"Sorry, Sheriff. Force of habit."

A wizened old-timer stood on tiptoes, craning to see over the shoulders of others hemming him in.

He said, "Is it is, or is it ain't?"

"It's gold," Highgrade said.

A collective sigh rose up.

"It's the mother lode. Richest gold-bearing rock these old eyes of mine have ever seen," Highgrade said.

"You go along with that, Bissell?" someone said.

"Based on a preliminary inspection, first impressions only, mind you, I'd have to say that I need a second look," Bissell said.

He took the rock away from Highgrade. "It looks good," he admitted.

Somebody hoo-rahed. One of the ranch hands drew his gun and fired it into the air. That so irked Larch that he rushed the man, pulling his own gun and laying the barrel hard across the other's forehead.

Knocked out, the cowboy sagged against his partner, who held him and kept him from falling. Larch pistol-whipped him, too, and the duo splashed down together into the mud.

No other immediate opportunities for head-clonking having presented themselves, the sheriff holstered his gun. Stalking over to Bissell, he tore the ore from his hands, repossessing it.

"Evidence," he said.

Bissell was not inclined to dispute the matter. He had other, more important things on his mind.

He said, "Where—where did it come from?"

"Beats me," Larch said.

He pointed to Slocum.

"There's the genius who killed the goose with the golden eggs," Larch said.

Slocum became the focus of the crowd's attention. Angry mutterings burbled up from their ranks. Drawing a last puff on his cigar, he took it from the corner of his mouth and flipped it at the front line that was pressing toward him. The cigar stub landed near the feet of the nearest citizens, splashing a burst of small orange embers before expiring with a hiss in the mud.

Switching the rifle to his left hand, he used his right to unlatch the leather thong looped over the top of his gun, freeing it for fast action if needed. The gesture was not lost on the citizens, who halted their forward motion in his direction.

He said, "I'll tell you this: The only gold that Ramey ever got was at gunpoint, and the closest he ever came to diggings is when he planted his victims in some lonely graves. He never did an honest day's work in his life. If you want to know where that gold came from, look for the buzzards. They'll lead you to the real finder of that gold, some prospector that Ramey robbed and killed."

George was red-faced with indignation.

"You sure he didn't tell you where the gold was? Maybe you killed him to keep the secret to yourself," he said.

"Mister, if I knew where the gold was, I'd be long gone from here, heading for the strike to stake my claim," Slocum said.

That made sense, since it's what anyone else would have done if they had been in possession of the secret.

Slocum pointed to the mountain ramparts walling off the western horizon.

"It's up there someplace, just waiting to be found," he said.

That took the focus off him and put it back on the gold. The crowd, which had verged on becoming a mob, was now atomized into a mass of self-serving gold seekers.

Amid the hubbub, various schemes were hatched for finding the gold:

Search the dead man for any map, claim, or written instructions concerning the location of the find that he might have on his possession. Follow the tracks his horse had made in the wet ground to trail it backward to the lode. Was the horse stolen? If so, the identity of its owner might furnish a clue. Examine the ore for any clues to the geological strata and land forms from which it came. Look for buzzards scavenging the remains of the original finder, as Slocum had suggested. These and a baker's dozen other ideas, each progressively more farfetched than the last, were floated up by the citizens of Blue Meadow.

A few self-starting direct actionists jumped the gun by quietly melting away from the crowd, saddling their horses, and riding south out of town, backtracking Ramey's trails. The sight of them galvanized those left behind. Some mounted up and followed in pursuit; others, more farsighted, formed alliances to organize and outfit more systematic gold-hunting expeditions.

Tempers flared at the discovery that George and his fellow merchants had already raised prices on their wares in anticipation of the sudden demand. Those prices were met, though not without harsh words. The first in line grumbled but they paid, knowing that if they passed up the opportunity to buy now, those behind them would not hesitate.

The sun was edging the mountains when Slocum finally rode out of Blue Meadow. The town disgorged its inhabitants, spilling them out on the road south toward its junction with the Bearclaw Trail into the hills. The rush was on.

Slocum rode north to claim his bounty, but he would soon return.

Slocum took the corpse to Palmer Lake, where there was a railroad station. He wired to Denver, alerting his contact in the D&RG hierarchy that he had bagged Ramey. Slocum had worked for the railroad before. They knew him, and they knew that if he said something was so, then it was so. They sent a special express down the line to Palmer Lake to pick up him and the body. The local station master was mightily impressed.

Slocum rode in a baggage car with the corpse. When the train was out of sight of the station, Slocum used his rifle to shoot at the telegraph lines running parallel to the tracks. Winchester slugs shattered the insulators securing the lines to the poles, cutting the wires so that they fell to the ground.

The telegraph at Palmer Lake was the nearest Western Union office to Blue Meadow. By cutting the lines, he made sure that the news about the gold strike would not flash ahead of him to Denver and set off the rush before he had a chance to take advantage of it.

The train arrived in Denver before sundown. Pettibone, the railroad agent, came aboard and identified the corpse from a wanted circular in his possession. He was authorized to pay Slocum in cash on the spot and he did so.

Denver was a hell of a town with many temptations to part both the foolish and the wise from their money. Slocum had been on the trail for many days, but he resisted the lure of whiskey and women long enough to take care of business.

First, he went to a whiskey wholesaler's, a warehouse where the fumes of alcohol were strong enough to bring tears to a man's eyes. Slocum had a powerful thirst, but this was business. He bought and paid for a wagonload of whiskey. Rotgut whiskey, which he bought cheap and planned to sell dear. It was as much trouble to transport a load of good stuff into the mountains as a load of swill, and the thirsty gold seekers who would soon be swarming into the Kettle wouldn't care about the difference. He had been in enough gold rushes to know that the real money came from the prospectors and not from prospecting. He arranged with the manager to take delivery of the wet goods at first light of the following day.

Mules were better than horses for hauling a heavy load. He bought a string of mules, harnesses, a freight wagon, feed stores for the animals, and other necessities from various outfitters. Last but not least, he bought some supplies for himself, including food and plenty of guns and ammunition.

Everything was set for his departure at tomorrow dawn, when he would take his outfit on the road. In the meantime, he had money in his pocket and a night to kill in Denver.

First, he bought himself a steak dinner with all the trimmings, including two bottles of good redeye. He drank one bottle with dinner and took the other with him. Having fed the inner man, he set out to satisfy other hungers.

The town was filled with whores but he wanted something high class. That necessitated that he clean up his own act. Weeks in the saddle had left him more than a little ripe. He bought himself some new clothes, then had a hot bath, a shave, and a haircut. When the bathhouse attendant asked him what he wanted done with his old clothes, Slocum told him to burn them.

He killed the second bottle before setting off for a fancy house. He was not drunk, but was feeling no pain. Just to be on the safe side, he picked up another bottle before starting on his rounds. He'd drink the genuine, bottled-in-bond article instead of the watered-down variety sold in the houses. It struck him as funny that here he was, the owner of a wagonload of whiskey, buying a bottle of booze from a retailer. But that barrel rotgut was for selling, not drinking, and besides, it was safely locked up in the warehouse until tomorrow morn.

The house was a handsome structure in a quiet part of town, with a pillared front and stained-glass fanlight over the door. Piano music mingled with murmured conversation, drifting through open windows into the cool night air. An unseen night bird chirped in the trees.

The doorman at first looked askance at allowing entry to a rough-looking hombre like Slocum, until he saw the color of the man's money. Then he let him in with as much enthusiasm as if he were admitting a bank president. More, considering the shaky finances of some of the city's banks.

The madame was Mrs. Fotheringale, a woman with the looks and physique of a dish-faced bear. She escorted Slocum into the parlor, where the "gentlemen" received the "ladies."

He paused on the threshold to survey the room, scanning it for unfriendly faces. Over the years, he'd made a lot of enemies. Most of them were dead, but sometimes they had vengeful kinfolk or associates. But he saw no threat in the men in the parlor, who had eyes only for the parade of fine female flesh on display.

About a half-dozen whores promenaded in the parlor. They were young, good-looking, well built, clean, and fresh. A few others were busy upstairs with "gentlemen friends." House custom was for each of the whores to be introduced to a newcomer, so he could see them all before settling on his pick.

The madame said, "Just sing out when something strikes your fancy."

"I know what to do," Slocum said. "I've been to the fair before."

"I'll bet you have, cowboy."

The procession of whores put fire in his blood. Mariah was the one that he had to have. Mariah—that's what she called herself. Maybe it was her real name, maybe it wasn't. What difference did it make?

She was a big brunette with an hourglass shape. Dark, with some Spanish blood in her or maybe Indian. Thick masses of inky-black hair, almond-shaped dark eyes, a wide triangular face with prominent cheekbones, and a full-lipped red mouth. Her skin was the color of old gold, and there was plenty of it showing in the low-cut red satin dress. Broad shoulders supported heavy breasts with deep cleavage. She didn't smile overmuch, which pleased him. A whore's smile is fool's gold.

After Slocum made his choice known, Mrs. Fotheringale handled the finances. The freight and handling charges were top dollar, but Slocum didn't kick. He knew that in women, as in all else, you get what you pay for.

He followed Mariah out of the parlor, into the main hall.

"Plan to be in town long, Mr. Slocum?" she said.

"I'm in Denver for a one-night layover. I want to get laid, so I'm staying over for a night."

"Well, you came to the right place, and the right gal."

"I don't doubt it."

She climbed the grand staircase to the second floor. Slocum was right behind, eyeing her behind. Her bottom was ripe and round, making a big circle against the back of her tight red dress. Her buttocks twitched and her hips swayed as she went up the steps. There was a tightness in the pit of Slocum's stomach as that succulent ass shimmied in front of his face. He chewed the corner of his mustache.

The room was on the left at the end of the hall. Mariah lit a lamp and lowered the flame.

"Not too dark," Slocum said. "I want to look at you."

"Look all you like. You're paying for it," she said.

Slocum unbuckled his gunbelt and hung it over one of the knobs at the head of the brass bedstead. Mariah raised an eyebrow but said nothing.

"I don't like to have my hand too far from a gun. A personal peculiarity of mine," Slocum said.

"Mister, I'm an expert on the personal peculiarities of men. If that's what makes you happy, be my guest. It won't cost you nothing extra."

"Much obliged."

Slocum embraced her. Beneath the smooth skin and the soft roundness there was a fine, well-toned physique. That suited Slocum. He made love the same way he did everything else, at full tilt and don't spare the horses, and he appreciated a partner who could go the distance.

She leaned into him. Her hair smelled sweet and her flesh smelled sweeter. Her skin was smoother than the satin dress he was peeling her out of.

The dress rustled as it was removed. It pooled at her feet. She wore black ankle boots with pointed toes and high heels. She stepped out of the dress. She wore a white shift with a flaring skirt and a white ribbed waist cincher over it. The cincher plumped up her breasts and bottom.

Slocum rubbed her breasts, squeezing them. He pulled down her shoulder straps and freed her breasts from the cups, baring them. They were full with wide dark nipples. He nuzzled them, hands creeping down her back to fasten on her ass cheeks, kneading them.

The crotch of his pants tented outward. She put her hands against his hardness, rubbing it.

"I see you didn't check all your guns," she said.

"You check it."

She unfastened his pants, freeing him.

"Lord, that's a whopper," she said.

He put his hand on the back of her neck and pushed her head down. "Give it a get-acquainted kiss," he said.

"You didn't pay for that," she said.

"I will."

"In advance."

He was eager but she was adamant. Grumbling, he dug some money out of his pockets, forking it over.

"That's too much. You overpaid," she said.

"That's in advance of any other extras I might want that's not on the going rate."

"Suit yourself."

"That's what I'm trying to do."

She knelt on the bed with her legs folded under her, ass perched on the backs of her heels. Licking her lips, she leaned forward, her breasts dangling. Slocum fit himself into her mouth, stretching it, breathing hard from deep in the pit of his belly as her seething sleekness enveloped him. He put his hand on her head, guiding its bobbing movements. His other hand pinched her nipples until they were sore and hard. He came fast, feeding her a mouthful.

He'd figured on that. He'd been a long time without a woman and was bound to be short-fused on the first go-round. Now that he had let off some steam, he geared up for the long pull. He kept himself in her mouth, still thick and swollen. He pulled the bottle cork with his teeth and guzzled raw whiskey. Heat spread through belly and loins, making him hard again.

He pulled out of her mouth and put her on her back. He lifted her skirt. Under it she wore a pair of petticoats and bloomers. He raised the former and lowered the latter. Her ripe-lipped sex was furred with a thick black bush.

Spreading her legs, he got between them. Her legs folded, hugging his sides. He rubbed her between the legs, then snaked his longhorn into her. Her eyes rolled up in her head when he was in deep. Then he put it to her, riding hard and fast. This time he was a Slo-cum.

Afterward, he drank more whiskey. Then he put it to her again.

In the morning, as the sun lifted up into a cloudless sky, Slocum left Denver. He was feeling a far sight better than when he'd arrived.

2

Julian Roux did his digging for gold with a deck of cards. He was a gambler. So was the man who sat opposite him at the card table, Blackie Hawkins. They were the last two players left in a marathon high-stakes poker game in a private room on the second floor of the Savoy Club in San Francisco's notorious Barbary Coast.

A lamp with a tasseled shade hung on a rope stretching down from the ceiling, throwing a cone of yellow light down on the green baize table in the center of the room. Tobacco smoke hung thick in the air, heavy, curling. Walls paneled with wooden wainscoting and red and black satin wallpaper muffled the clamor of the gamblers, drinkers, and skirt-chasers thronging the ground floor of the club tonight as they did every night, seven days a week.

This private room was reserved for the big-money high rollers. Earlier tonight, eight had taken a seat at that green table, anteing up two thousand dollars each for the privilege of sitting in on the game. Now, hours later, as midnight neared, all but two of those players had been winnowed out. The last hand of the game was being played, with an eighteen-thousand-dollar jackpot at hand for the winner.

Three of the original players had slunk off earlier after being busted out of the game; three remained to see the outcome of this final hand of cards that had proved too rich for their blood. The observers sat as still and motionless as worshipers at silent prayer.

Julian Roux was doing some silent praying of his own. No sign of tension showed on his blandly expressionless face. He was in his early thirties, a midsize man with wavy brown hair, dark eyes, and smooth pale skin unaccustomed to daylight. A high forehead and alert eyes denoted an active intelligence. Twin knobs of knotted muscle stood out at the hinges of his jaw. He wore a brown suit trimmed with dark brown piping, white shirt, and elegant Spanish boots. A diamond stickpin adorned his gray silk cravat; the heavy gold chain of his watch fob showed against his vest. The stickpin and the gold watch represented the sum total of wealth in his possession; every cent he owned was anted into the pot.

Blackie Hawkins was equally calm and unruffled, at least on the surface. If not the King of the Barbary Coast, he was one of its barons. The owner of the Savoy, he boasted that he and his associates had left behind a dead man for every nail that had gone into the building of his gambling hall. It was no idle brag. A gunfighter and killer, he was the leader of a gang of other gunfighters and killers that had plied their trade up and down the California coast.

A fine figure of a man, he was gifted with rugged good looks, a muscular physique, iron nerves, and lightning reflexes. Jet-black hair that came down in a widow's peak had given rise to his nickname. An immaculate midnight-black suit was offset by a snow-white shirt garnished with lace trimmings at throat and cuffs. His only item of personal adornment was a black onyx stone set in a gold ring that he wore on the thumb of his left hand. When he changed position in his chair, a pistol could be glimpsed under his jacket on his left side. No fancy gambler's derringer this, but rather a long-barreled six-gun with black horn handles that was tucked into the top of his waistband butt-out to facilitate a cross-belly draw.

"Call," he said.

Julian turned over his cards. "Three queens," he said.

Hawkins showed his hand. His high cards were three kings.

The observers at the table visibly sagged with the relief of tension. Neither Hawkins nor Julian batted an eye.

"Well, that cleans me out," Julian said.

Hawkins shrugged, flashing a brilliant white-toothed grin that did not reach up to his eyes.

"Luck of the draw," he said.

"Bad luck—for me," Julian said. He smiled, too.

Hawkins left the pot on the table, untouched. It would keep.

Chair legs scraped floorboards as the players got up from the table. The others said their good-byes and went out, leaving Hawkins and Julian alone in the room.

"I thought you had me there for a while," Hawkins said.

"So did I. That's why I bet the farm," Julian said.

"You're not cut out to be a farmer, anyhow."

"Or a gambler, looks like."

"It's not so easy when you're playing with your own money."

"You were."

"Sure, but I've got a lot more of it than you."

"You do now."

"Buy you a drink?"

"Don't mind if I do," Julian said.

Hawkins crossed to the sideboard, where he filled two shot glasses with whiskey from a cut-crystal decanter. Julian joined him. They raised their glasses.

"Luck," Hawkins toasted.

"I could use some," Julian said.

He noted with some satisfaction that his hand betrayed not a tremor.

The duo tossed back their drinks. The whiskey might have been water for all the effect it had on Julian, who barely noticed it going down.

Hawkins said, "Well, what now?"

"Now I start all over again," Julian said.

"Why don't you come back to work for me?"

"Dealing, or shooting?"

"Whichever you prefer, or both."

Julian shook his head. "Thanks, but no."

That set Hawkins to shaking his head. "Still determined to strike out on your own, eh, Julian?"

"Something like that."

"You see where it's brought you so far."

"Luck of the draw."

"No, it's more than that. You're as good a cardplayer as any I've seen, but that's not enough. If I lost, I could have gone to the safe and taken out a few piles of greenbacks and got back in the game. That gives me the confidence to crowd my luck, push it to the limit. You bet everything but your shirt. That's got to affect your play, no matter how savvy you are. It's like the late war: The Rebs didn't lack for nerve and skill, but the Yanks had them beat in manpower and material by about five to one. All things being equal, the North was bound to win in the long run, which it did."

"Maybe so, Blackie, but we gave those bluebellies one hell of a scrap while it lasted."

"Sure, but I'm talking about winning, not losing gallantly."

"If you have to lose, that's the way to do it," Julian said.

He got his hat, fitted it on his head. "I've taken up enough of your time for one night. Now, I'll be on my way," he said.

"That offer of mine still stands. I'd like to have you back working for me."

"Dealing? Or shooting?"

"Just dealing, if you've lost your taste for gunplay."

"You know I don't shy from trouble, Blackie—"

"I do know it."

"—but that last go-round we were on was kind of raw."

"Well . . . that's the way of the world, kid. I didn't like it any better than you, but what choice did I have? If I didn't do it, someone else would, and then my friends at City Hall wouldn't be my friends anymore."

"I'm not passing judgment. You've got to do what you've got to do. So do I."

"Damned straight, Julian. Still, you're going to have to build a stake somehow, and I'd hate to think of you shearing the lambs for some other outfit. If you're going to play cards, you might as well play them for the Savoy, where you belong."

"Just cards?"

"Just cards."

"I appreciate the offer, Blackie, but—"

Hawkins held up his hands to silence the other.

"Don't make up your mind now. Sleep on it, and tell me your decision tomorrow," he said.

"I'll do that," Julian said.

"Good man!"

Hawkins clapped Julian on the back.

"Of course, if you change your mind about the guns, that wouldn't exactly break my heart, either. I'd hate to lose one of my Pallbearers."

"We'll see, Blackie."

"Fine. You can even pick the jobs you want to go on. If you don't like the smell of them, you can pass with no hard feelings. Nobody else working for me has that choice, so that shows how much I like you."

"Thanks. I'll let you know."

"You'll come around, Julian. What else are you going to do, work for a living?"

"Lord, no!"

They crossed to the door. As Julian reached for the handle, a knock sounded from outside.

"It's me, boss—Schlemmer," a voice said.

Hawkins nodded. Julian opened the door. Schlemmer stood in the hall, a stocky older man with sleek lead-colored hair combed straight back and a handsome pair of mustachios of the same color. Like his boss, he wore somber black formal wear and a white shirt. A bulge showed under his coat on his right hip where his gun was. He was one of Hawkins's permanent cadre of six deadly gunslingers, the Pallbearers.

He and Julian exchanged nods.

"This isn't your night, Roux," Schlemmer said.

"Bad news travels fast," Julian said.

"So should you. Some friends of yours are waiting outside for you in front of the club."

"A man without money has no friends, Schlemmer."

"Come to think of it, they don't look too friendly at that."

Hawkins said, "What's cooking, Schlemmer?"

"Trouble, boss. Clipper Shays and some of his crew are laying for brother Julian here. Or is that ex-brother?"

"It's whatever you want it to be, Schlemmer," Julian said.

"You're the one who wanted out."

"Which is where I'm going, if you'll be so good as to step aside."

"Hold on a second," Hawkins said. "Quit baiting him, Schlemmer."

"I don't mind," Julian said.

"Sure, he can take it. He's a big boy," Schlemmer said.

"Shut up. Now, what's this about you and Shays, Julian?"

"I needed to build up my stake for tonight's game, so I took some of Clipper's money."

"How much?"

"Plenty."

"He claims you cheated," Schlemmer said.

"He didn't say that to my face last night when he lost."

"He must've thought you were still part of the outfit. Today he learns different, so he comes gunning for you. He always was a sore loser," Hawkins said.

"Could be," Julian said.

"He wouldn't have dared bracing you when you were one of us, but now that you've gone off by yourself, he must figure that a lone man is easy pickings."

"Then I'll have to disabuse him of that notion."

"He's waiting for you to try," Schlemmer said.

"That wharf rat wouldn't have the nerve to come alone. How many are with him, Schlemmer?" Hawkins asked.

"I made it about four or five, boss. But it's hard to tell, it's so foggy out there tonight."

Schlemmer turned to Julian.

"You could sneak out the back and maybe get away in the fog," he said.

"What, and spoil the party?" Julian said.

"That's the stuff," Hawkins said.

He went to a cabinet, opening it. It was filled with various makes and calibers of handguns hanging on hooks. He took a long-barreled revolver and offered it to Julian.

"Thanks, I've already got a gun."

"Have another. What the hell, it's a party, isn't it?"

"All right. Thanks," Julian said.

Taking the gun, he broke it, making sure it was loaded.

"I'll give it back when I'm done," he said.

Hawkins waved a hand. "Keep it. I've got plenty more," he said.

Julian stuck the gun in the top of his pants, covering it with his coat.

Hawkins said, "Looks like your vacation from gunplay was a short one. Only this time, you have to shoot for free."

"That's all right. Putting a bullet in Clipper will be a positive pleasure."

"Careful, Julian. Clipper throws plenty of weight on the docks. He's got some powerful friends at City Hall. They won't like it if you kill him," Hawkins said.

"*I* won't like it if he kills me."

"He'd slink off like a whipped cur if you were back in the outfit again."

"If I counted on that, you wouldn't want me back."

"True enough."

"I'll be on my way. Mustn't keep Clipper waiting."

"Luck, kid. Shoot straight."

Julian started out. Schlemmer had to step aside to let him pass. Julian acknowledged him with a cool nod.

He said, "About coming back—I'll let you know tomorrow."

"I'll be waiting," Hawkins said.

Julian went down the hall, toward the landing. Hawkins stepped into the passageway, watching him go. Julian rounded the corner without looking back. When he was out of view, Schlemmer flipped him a mock-ironic salute.

"Auf Wiedersehn," he said.

"Want to bet?" Hawkins said.

Schlemmer looked at Hawkins, studying his face, which gave away nothing. "You serious, boss?"

"I'm always serious about money."

Schlemmer shook his head. "He hasn't got a chance. He lost his guts on the last job out."

"I say different. How much do you want to bet on it?"

"A hundred."

"Make it five."

Schlemmer pursed his lips. "A hundred is all I'll go, boss."

"Five hundred's too rich for your blood, eh?"

"If it was anyone else, I'd go five. But with your talent for picking sure things, I don't want to stick my neck out. A hundred is all I'll risk."

"Done," Hawkins said.

Looking both ways to make sure they were alone in the hall, Hawkins tilted his head toward Schlemmer and spoke, low-voiced.

"Clipper doesn't know that it was me who set up brother Julian for him?"

"Not to worry, boss. I made the rounds of the grog shops and dives earlier today, dropping the word in the right ears that Roux was quits with us and that none of the outfit would lift a finger to help him. I also made sure to mention that he'd be here tonight, just like you told me to do."

"Good."

"I told everyone I talked to that they were getting the inside lowdown, that it was in the strictest of confidence, and that they weren't to tell a living soul. Naturally, the news was all over the waterfront before sundown. No one can trace it back to us."

"Good, good."

Schlemmer frowned, puzzled. "I don't get it, boss. You put Julian on the spot so Clipper's gang will finish him off, but you bet that they won't."

"They won't."

"That's what I don't get."

"Ordeal by fire, Schlemmer."

"You've lost me."

"Brother Roux thought he could run with the pack and not get dirty. After that last job, he learned better. Now, his conscience bothers him and he doesn't like that."

"Like I said, he turned yellow, lost his guts."

"No, Schlemmer, he just thinks too much. But when Clipper's bunch starts coming at him, he won't have time to think. Just shoot, or die."

"And if he dies . . . ?"

"I'm out a hundred dollars," Hawkins said.

3

Julian paused at the mezzanine rail, looking down at the main floor of the Savoy Club. It was well past midnight but business was brisk. At the opposite end of the hall was a small stage where dancing girls and the occasional variety acts did their turns. It was empty now. The "dancers" doubled as hostesses and were scattered throughout the tables facing the stage, enticing customers to buy them drinks. The clientele was made up mostly of sailors, stevedores, and other waterfront types, although there was a leavening of well-dressed society swells who had come down from their Nob Hill mansions in search of illicit thrills—a dangerous proposition, which no doubt added to the excitement.

Half the floor was filled by the tables and chairs; the other half was taken up with games of chance: keno, faro, chuck-a-luck, and all the other lures by which men were divested of their money. The games were honest, more or less—meaning no dealer had ever been caught cheating. The saloon girls were required to cajole the customers to buy them drinks while the premises were open. What private arrangements they made after hours was their business. Two long bars served quantities of whiskey, wine, and beer; some of it was almost drinkable. Among Barbary Coast establishments, the Savoy was a paragon. As a well-respected gang leader Blackie Hawkins could afford to run an honest deal at his club.

Standing at the rail, Julian hatched out a plan and searched for someone to carry it out. Spying a likely prospect, he went downstairs to meet him.

Bill King was a good-natured dockside tough, more rowdy

than vicious. Catching his eye, Julian beckoned to him on the sidelines. King slipped away from the bar, joining him.

Julian had some loose change in his pockets and his lucky twenty-dollar gold piece, that was all. He showed the gold piece to King.

"How'd you like to earn this, Bill?"

"Sure. How?"

Julian told him the plan.

"That's all you want me to do? And you'll pay me twenty dollars for that?"

"That's right, Bill."

"Keep your money. I'll do that for laughs."

"Thanks, Bill. You're a pal."

"Forget it. When do we go?"

"Now, if you're ready."

"Sure. This'll be a good one on Clipper!"

"I hope so," Julian said.

They parted, King heading for a side door, Julian going to the main entrance.

Somewhere, a clock struck one, its tolling bell muffled by night and the cold, clammy fog rolling in off the bay, blanketing the waterfront.

The Savoy fronted a cobblestoned square. Opposite it was the back of a row of warehouse buildings. The club's facade suggested something of a cross between a Greek temple and a bank. It boasted four gold pillars. They were false pillars, gilded wood that bore no weight but were strictly decorative. A three-sided stone stairway led down to the sidewalk. A line of horse-drawn carriages stretched along the curb. The drivers stood alongside them, smoking, pacing, fortifying themselves against the chill with the occasional nip from a pocket flask. A club patron could hire one of these cabs with the assurance that they would not be waylaid and robbed, the drivers having a private arrangement to that effect with Hawkins. The few bold ones who ignored that prohibition were killed and left out in the open as a warning to others. Consequently, violations were few. This immunity from theft and worse was restricted to the cabs that picked up and discharged fares at the Savoy.

Passengers boarding hire-cabs outside its immediate vicinity did so at their own risk.

The gambling hall's well-lighted facade was veiled by mist. Beyond its gauzy glow, the square was dark, obscure. The fog was half rain, half mist. Cobblestones were beaded with moisture. Rifts yawned in the fog banks, allowing the tall masts of sailing ships to be glimpsed between the warehouses and above their roofs. The salty tang of brine hung in the wet air.

Like wolves lurking just beyond a campfire light, Clipper Shays's crew skulked in the shadows of the square, waiting for Julian Roux.

Shays himself was a brute, a bully, and sadist. He took his name not from the magnificent clipper ships playing their trade throughout the world's ports, but rather from his knack of "clipping" his luckless victims of all they owned, including, frequently, their lives. Smuggler, hijacker, oyster pirate, wrecker, receiver of stolen cargoes, strongarm, murderer—if there was a dirty dollar to be made on or near the water, he was game for it. Strong rumor had it that he was an inshore mariner who had never been out on blue water.

His signature yachtsman's cap was pulled low, its visor shielding his eyes from the drizzle. He had taken it from a crewman he had shot during a botched robbery attempt aboard a ferry boat. A brace of pistols were thrust into the pockets of his navy pea coat, whose collar was turned up against the damp.

With him were his followers, piratical rogues, the sweepings of the fo'c'sle. Lew, the first mate, blue-jowled and sly-eyed; Carl, his weaselly kid brother; Hooky, whose right hand, torn off by a snagged line on a ship cruising the Alaskan seas, had been replaced by a wickedly curved steel hook, shaped like a question mark. Red, glum except when drunk, when he was roaring terror; McGruff, a nightmare figure, six and a half feet of dim hulking malice.

All were armed with guns, knives, and blunt objects, in various combinations.

They knew to steer clear of Hawkins's domain. To transgress his boundaries would bring swift and massive retaliation.

So, they hovered at the outskirts, covering the exits, waiting for their prey.

The Savoy faced west. Opposite it, on the other side of the square, was Shays, Red, and McGruff. Carl and Hooky covered the north side; Lew scouted the south.

Each time someone exited through the front doors, Shays started forward, reaching for his guns, only to back off when Julian Roux failed to appear.

A foghorn hooted. Shays sneezed.

"Damn that lubber!" he said, cursing.

He and Red were big, solid men, but McGruff dwarfed them. Stolid, impassive, inert, McGruff had the fearlessness of near imbecility.

In the corner of his eye, Shays saw Red edge off to the side, making furtive movements accompanied by a sloshing sound. He lashed out, cuffing Red's ear, jolting him.

Red cried out. A pint bottle flew from his hands, skittering across the stones from the force of the blow, but not breaking.

"No grog!" Shays said. "You need a clear head for this job."

"I wasn't drinking to get drunk, I was just having a little nip to warm my bones," Red said.

"I'll roast you on a spit, you blasted soak!"

Red rubbed his ear and the side of his head.

Shays took a few steps to the right, peering into the murk at the south side of the square.

"Where's Lew? I don't see him . . . Confound this fog!" Shays said.

He continued in that direction for another half-dozen paces before he spied Lew, a solitary figure who emerged from a dark, recessed doorway at his approach.

He said, "What's up, Clipper?"

"You tell me."

"Nothing, yet."

"Keep a sharp watch, Lew."

"Aye."

Turning, Shays crossed the square in the opposite direction until he saw Hooky and Carl. They stood at the northeast corner. They came out into the open as Shays neared. He waved them back into place before returning to his previous vantage point.

Hooky and Carl had been teamed to offset each other's weaknesses. Hooky was a good man but minus a hand. Carl had two good hands but he was green, untried.

They stood facing south. Hoofbeats clip-clopped behind them, from the north. Clattering wheels, creaking harnesses, the chuffing breath of the horses.

This was nothing new. Carriages had been arriving and departing at the Savoy with lulling regularity. The newcomer did the unexpected by reining to a halt at the roadside about a stone's throw north of the square.

Hooky and Carl turned to look at it. A private carriage, yoked to a single team of horses in tandem. Fog blurred its edges. Black, with a dim yellow lamp on a front side corner. Red curtains hid the interior. The driver sat up on the box, a featureless man-shaped outline.

Carl said, "What do you make of that?"

"I don't know," Hooky said.

Having a steel claw for a hand made reloading a difficult task. Hooky held one gun in his hand and kept another in his coat pocket. His gun arm was folded across his chest, hiding the weapon under the front of his coat.

Frowning, he scratched his head, a ticklish proposition when a steel hook is employed for the purpose.

He said, "Look sharp for the gambler! If he gets by us, Clipper will have our guts for breakfast. I'll see what this coach is about."

Carl went back to watching for Julian Roux. Hooky went north, drawing abreast of the carriage on the other side of the street.

One of the team pawed the cobbles with its foreleg, jingling the harness rigging. Undercarriage springs squeaked.

The driver wore a shapeless slouch hat and a greatcoat thrown over his shoulders, buttoned at the throat and worn cape style. He was square-jawed, with pointed ears and bushy muttonchop whiskers. A hand rested on the sawed-off shotgun stretched across his lap.

He eyed Hooky, Hooky eyed him.

A hand lifted the curtain of the carriage's side window—a woman's hand, slim, pale, elegant. A dark-eyed face, otherwise featureless in the dimness, filled the window.

The woman spoke briefly to the driver. Hooky could hear the music of her voice but not the words. She ended on an interrogative note, so presumably she was asking a question. The driver's reply was curt, monosyllabic. He never took his eyes off Hooky.

Hooky wasn't sure what he had expected to find, but whatever it was, this wasn't it. Fading back, he drifted out of point-blank range of the shotgun before turning his back on it. He rejoined Carl on the corner.

"Well?" Carl said.

"Nothing to do with us. It's a lady."

"No lady'd be out at this time of night, Hooky. She's a whore. She good-looking?"

"I guess so."

"Must be. She didn't get to ride in that fancy rig being ugly. Probably waiting to meet her gentleman friend. I'd sure like to get a look at her."

"Ask her chaperone to introduce you. He's the fellow with the sawed-off shotgun," Hooky said.

Carl sniffed. "She's not the only whore around. Think I'll have me one after we get the gambler."

A thought struck Carl. "Hey, you don't think she could be waiting for *him*, do you, Hooky?"

"Waiting for Roux? 'Taint likely. If he could afford a fancy gal like that, he wouldn't have needed to clip Clipper for his roll," Hooky said.

"My aunt Tillie could beat Clipper at cards, and so could yours."

"If Clipper hears you say that, not even your brother Red could save you."

"Think I'm crazy enough to tell him the truth? That he can't play cards worth a thimbleful of wind?"

"That's not what this is all about."

"No? How do you see it, Hooky?"

"Clipper doesn't like losing, but he wasn't fired up until he heard that Roux was quits with Blackie. Whoever kills the gambler gets the rep. Now that he's playing a lone hand, lots of folks will go gunning for him. Clipper's going to get him first, and the rep that goes with it."

"I wouldn't mind if some of that rep rubs off on me."

"Me neither, Carl."

Gunfire erupted around them.

Bill King climbed out of a back window and doubled back around to the front, sneaking through the grounds on the north side of the Savoy. Light shining through the windows overhead splintered into shafts due to the prismatic effect of the fog. Tree trunks glistened; leaves dripped.

Keeping to the shadows, screened by shrubs, King crept toward the street. Wet grass cushioned his footfalls. He moved low, in a crouch.

Through a gap in the bushes he saw two men. They were on the other side of the iron spear fence surrounding the property. Their attention was divided between the grounds and the square. They were unaware of King, an accomplished footpad.

He stood on one knee behind a waist-high ornamental stone wall. The two men's faces were masked by shadows. King had spent enough time on similar street-corner vigils to know that that's what they were doing.

He drew his gun, a short-barreled, big-bore revolver. The front sight post was filed off so it wouldn't snag on the lining of his pocket. He could have shot both men dead in a trice, but that wasn't what Roux wanted. Roux just wanted him to make a fuss as a diversion. Not that King hadn't killed men for a gold double eagle before. He'd murdered for a lot less than that—for free, at times. But Roux wasn't looking for anyone else to fight his battles, he just wanted a distraction to confuse the foe and even up the odds.

Of course, King had to have some fun, too. He threw some lead in the general direction of the duo, not hitting them but coming damned close. A trick of the acoustics made the gun blasts boom like an artillery barrage.

Hooky ducked one of the stone pillars reinforcing the spear

fence. Carl threw himself flat on the cobbles.

"It's him! Dirty, murdering son—get him, Hooky!"

Carl and Hooky fired into the grounds. Even if they had struck the place where the shots came from, they would have missed King because he had already rolled a half-dozen paces away from it. But they weren't even close. Bullets holed leaves, snipped twigs. A slug thunked into a tree, spraying pulp and sap.

"I think I got him!" Carl said.

Guns drawn, Shays, Red, and McGruff dashed into the light of the square. Lew came running up from the south side.

Hooky and Carl kept firing, lines of light spearing from their gun barrels. Reports popped.

Shays ran toward them, the others following. Red paced him, careful not to pass him. McGruff trotted, heavy-footed. Lew brought up the rear, fast closing the distance between him and the trio.

As Lew drew abreast of the Savoy, Julian Roux stepped out from behind a gilt pillar and shot him.

Julian stood like a duelist, his gun arm extended straight out from his side. He wielded the six-gun that Hawkins had given him.

Glimpsing Julian in the corner of his eye, Lew faltered. A bullet tagged him during that split second of hesitation. It made a meaty thwacking sound going in.

Lew spun, fell, rolled, lay still.

The drivers idling on the pavement scattered. Spooked horses started kicking against the traces, nickering, uprearing.

Julian went down the stone stairway.

Shays, Red, and McGruff turned at the sound of gunfire behind them. They opened fire, cruel faces underlit by muzzle flares.

Julian was at street level, screened by the row of cabs.

"Get him, Red!" cried Shays.

Red was the best shot of the crew.

"Where is he? I can't see him!" Red said.

McGruff charged, wasting no words.

Julian clung to the side of the coach at the head of the

line. He dropped a shot into the curb, gouging out a chunk of pavement, spraying the horses with stinging stone chips.

The team stampeded, catapulting the driverless vehicle away from the Savoy. Steel-shod hoofs struck sparks from the cobbles. The fear-crazed animals coursed across the square.

Shays and his two sidemen had to scramble to keep from being trampled by the runaway coach. When it passed them, Julian let go and dropped off the side.

He was going too fast to stay on his feet so he didn't try. His legs folded and he hit the stones rolling, shoulders and upper arms absorbing most of the impact. He skidded to a stop and lay prone on the cobbles, gun in hand.

He shot Red first, drilling him through the middle. The slug raised a little puff of dust where it hit his shirt. Red back-pedaled. Julian shot him again. Red sat down hard, dead, slumping into a heap.

A slug shattered Shays's chest. He went to his knees, still holding his guns. Crumpling, he jerked the triggers, cratering the pavement.

McGruff kept coming, his empty gun clicking as he worked the trigger. He loomed large, blotting out the foreground.

Julian shot him. McGruff shuddered, shook it off, kept coming. Julian dropped the empty gun like a hot iron.

McGruff said, "I'll tear you apart—"

Reaching into his coat, Julian snaked out a four-barreled derringer, a lethal item known far and wide as a "pepperbox." He emptied it into McGruff, who came crashing down dead less than an arm's length away.

The runaway coach clattered past Hooky and Carl and kept on going. The man with the muttonchop whiskers had to fight to keep his team from succumbing to contagious panic flight.

Carl tried to reload, shaking so hard that he couldn't fit the rounds into the chamber. Gunshots in the square startled him into dropping his bullets, spilling them on the stones.

Hooky fired at Roux, missed. The prone man was hard to hit. Roux slithered toward Shays's discarded guns.

Starting toward him, Hooky stepped out from behind the cover of the square-sided fence post. Bill King recognized him. There was no mistaking him, not with that steel hook for a hand. King didn't have anything against him, but he didn't have anything for him, either. So, he shot him. Twice.

The first shot froze him in his tracks, the second felled him.

Carl had had enough. Abandoning his gun, he jumped up and ran. King was too disgusted to finish him off.

Melting into the darkness, King hopped the fence and absented himself from the vicinity, well pleased by his bit of fun.

Life still bubbled in Clipper Shays, though it was failing fast. He was shot through the lungs with a sucking chest wound. He tried to lift his guns but lacked the strength. Julian took them from him.

"You've run aground, Clipper."

"—four-flushing tinhorn . . . "

"The only cheating I did was against myself, to keep from winning your money too fast," Julian said.

Clipper's reply was choked off by a fit of coughing that brought up not words, but black blood.

"You lose again," Julian said.

He delivered the coup de grace, sending a bullet crashing through Shays's brain.

Julian was bruised, battered, winded. His clothes were torn. His hands, elbows, and knees were scraped, his left ankle was sore, but he was otherwise unharmed.

Rumblings from behind caused him to turn facing north. A two-horse black carriage rolled toward him at a moderate pace. He held both guns at the ready, not knowing how many rounds remained in each.

The carriage pulled up alongside him, halting. The driver, a stranger to Julian, kept both hands on the reins and pointedly stared ahead, as if to emphasize his unconnectedness with the violence that had just taken place.

The carriage door opened. Framed in the doorway was a woman, garbed and cloaked against the chill night air. A beauty she was, with dark eyes and full lips, her face coolly untroubled by the corpses strewn about at Julian's feet.

"Get in," she said.

The handsome equipage, the splendid horses, the woman's air of expensive refinement, all argued against any connection with Shays and his crew. They were worlds apart. Clipper lacked both the subtlety and the wherewithal for the carriage's apparition to be part of his murder plot.

The woman was alone in the carriage. Julian, shrugging, climbed inside, closing the door behind him. He sank into the cushioned seat opposite her just as the carriage started forward.

Hawkins and Schlemmer stood on a balcony overlooking the square from which they had watched the gunfight.

Hawkins said, "You owe me a hundred, Schlemmer."

"Roux had help! He didn't do it alone!"

"What of it? The bet didn't say anything about him having to gun the whole gang himself . . . which he did; all but one, anyhow. He'd've got Hooky, too, if it came to that. Pay up."

Schlemmer paid; muttering, but he paid.

The carriage, with Julian Roux inside it, drove to the end of the square, turned the corner, and disappeared down a side street, going east.

"Who was that, boss?"

"Damned if I know, Schlemmer. Find out."

"Right."

"And while you're at it, send a runner over to Pete Nilsson to tell him that Clipper's gone down with all hands."

"Nilsson'll be glad to hear that, boss. He hated Shays worse than anybody."

"I'll say. Hated him enough to pay me to kill him," Hawkins said.

Schlemmer, going indoors, paused in midstride.

"Come again, boss? Nilsson paid you to kill Clipper?"

"That's right. Actually, I broached the proposition to Pete, after first making sure that Clipper would come gunning for Julian. As long as there was going to be a killing, why not turn a profit on it?"

Hawkins patted the gun hidden beneath his coat.

"If Julian hadn't done for Clipper, I'd have finished the job myself. Pete Nilsson paid in advance and I had no intention of returning the money," he said.

"Smart thinking, boss. And I ask again: Who belonged to that carriage?"

"That I don't know, Schlemmer. And what I don't know, I don't like. Friends of Julian's, maybe . . . or maybe not. I'd hate to have his gun working for somebody else. Find out who it was," Hawkins said.

4

Whiskey on the wind; raw, pungent, invigorating—

Highgrade awoke, groaning. For a timeless time he had hung suspended in the borderland between sleep and wakefulness; now, he broke through the surface into awareness.

He lay still, unmoving, his eyes closed. Sleep was peace. Why, then, had he awakened?

Something tingled in his nostrils, tickling, tantalizing. What was it? The smell of whiskey. This, then, was what had brought him around.

He sat up, sending an avalanche of misery crashing down on himself. A red-hot railroad spike was being driven through the center of his brain. Each lurching heartbeat was a sledgehammer blow driving the spike deeper. He clamped his hands to the sides of his head to lessen the pounding. Lights flashed under his eyes.

Worse than that was his thirst. His mouth was parched, desert-dry. His lips were cracked. His tongue felt like a stunned, blackened stump. *Thirst.*

A coughing fit seized him, wracking him with heaving rheumy spasms that made his bones ache. He sobbed for breath, and each shuddering gasp was laced with the smell of whiskey.

Knuckling his gummy eyelids, he opened them and looked around.

Stone wall, dirt floor, wooden pallet. The pallet protruded from the wall like a shelf. Highgrade sat on it, leaning against the wall to keep from falling over. His legs hung over the side, feet dangling inches above the hard-packed dirt floor. The stones were cool where he pressed the side of his face against them. A long narrow window opened in the wall above his head, open but for the iron bars set in it.

More bars stood opposite the stone wall, about eight feet away. A gridwork of them, stretching from floor to ceiling, caging him.

Memory returned. Highgrade was in jail; the Blue Meadow jail, to be exact. He knew it well. This was not his first visit.

He was in a cell at the back of the one-story structure. Through the bars he could see clear to the front. He was alone. The sheriff's office proper, occupying the front half of the building, was deserted. The rifle rack was empty. Daylight shone through the open front windows and doorway.

Yet he smelled whiskey. Of that there could be no mistake. Highgrade could sniff out the stuff like a preacher could scent out sin.

Grasping the bars overhead, Highgrade hauled himself up to the window, which faced west.

Long blue shadows of early morning slanted across the prairie stretching out to the hazy front range. In the foreground stood a freight wagon harnessed to an eight-mule team. A man was watering the mules one by one, using a bucket he refilled from a muddy creek that ran a few dozen yards away from the back of the jail.

All these impressions, however, registered but dimly on Highgrade's mind. All but one: seated firmly in the wagon bed was a row of barrels, with wooden staves and iron hoops. They were covered by a tarpaulin, which was tied down to the sides of the wagon, though not without some gaps through which could be seen the barrels. What the tarp could not cover, though, was the smell of whiskey coming from those barrels.

A wagonload of whiskey!

Highgrade beheld the vision with no less wonder than the Argonauts of old beheld the Golden Fleece.

He tried to cry out, but could muster only a forlorn croak. So dry was he that he lacked enough saliva even to swallow.

Fighting panic, he took a deep breath. Winds blowing from the west carried whiskey-laden fumes to him. Taking several more breaths, he tasted the stuff with every lungful. Its restorative effect worked on him like smelling salts on a person in a swoon.

"For God's sake, mister, help!" he cried.

The wagon driver looked up, taking notice of Highgrade. No teamster he, but a cowboy, with a wide-brimmed hat, jeans, boots. The scissor tails of his duster coat dangled down near his heels. He held a wide wooden bucket up to the snout of one of the long-eared mules in his train, who drank noisily from it.

The stranger turned his attention away from Highgrade, and back to his task of watering the animals.

Highgrade tried again, thirst adding real desperation to his plea.

"Help me, mister, please!"

"Why?" said the stranger.

"I'm locked in, I can't get out!"

The stranger chuckled.

"Tell that to the sheriff," he said.

"I can't! The sheriff's gone! The deputy's gone, too! They've all gone off and forgotten to let me out!"

"People in jail usually have a good reason for being there."

"Not me, mister. I was just sleeping off a drunk, like I do all the time, only this time they've all gone off without letting me out! You don't want me to die in here, do you?"

"I don't have any strong feelings about it, one way or the other."

"That's not very neighborly, mister."

"Neither am I."

"Nor am I, so why don't you let me out?"

"I'm studying on it," the stranger said.

He took a good long look at the face framed in the jail window.

"Ain't you the one they call Highgrade?"

"Sure, sure, that's me! You know me, huh? Everybody knows old Highgrade!"

"Didn't recognize you without the mud," the stranger said.

"Huh?"

"Busting a man out of jail is serious business."

"Leaving him to die of hunger and thirst is serious, too!"

"Especially thirst, eh? Well, never mind. Sit tight," the stranger said.

From the back of the wagon, he took a smith's hammer and a prybar.

"If anyone starts messing with the wagon, holler," he said.

"Mister, I'll sing out like the heavenly choir!" said Highgrade.

The stranger walked around to the front of the building. There was no door. It had been removed from its hinges. The window shutters were likewise removed.

Sun shining at the stranger's back threw his long shadow across the jail floor as he crossed the threshold. He went to the back, where the cells were.

Reluctantly tearing his gaze away from the whiskey wagon, Highgrade climbed off the pallet and lurched toward the cage wall.

"Bless you!" he said.

He grabbed the cell door by the bars—it swung wide open. Surprised, he would have fallen had he not been clutching the bars.

"It's not locked," the stranger said.

Straightening up, while not releasing his grip on the bars for fear of losing his balance, Highgrade blinked owlishly.

"Well, what do you know? I never thought to try the door to see if it was locked or not. That's one on me, huh?"

"No, on me," the stranger said.

He turned and walked out. Highgrade started after him, stopped, went back into the cell to retrieve his hat, which lay upended on the dirt under the pallet. Grabbing it, he hurried outside.

Daylight punched him between the eyes. His knees buckled. Blindly he thrust out his hands, one of them striking the wall. He clung to it until the sinking spell passed. Hammering sounds continued. He shook his head to clear it but the hammering continued.

"I need a drink bad," he said.

Spots dancing before his eyes, he groped his way to the rear of the jail. The morning sun was not hot but bright, so bright that it was painful. It hurt less when he stood in the shadows. He still heard hammering, though.

The stranger was going about his business, tending to the mules.

Highgrade said, "What're you hauling, mister?"

"As if you didn't know!"

Highgrade could almost taste the whiskey. His mouth watering, he smacked his lips.

He said, "How about a snort?"

"Sure, what've you got?"

"No, no, I mean, how about you giving me a snort?"

"That's what I thought you meant," the stranger said. "I'll sell you one."

"How much?"

"Two bits a throw."

"How about one on the house?"

"How about jumping over the moon? I'm not running a charity here," the stranger said.

Knowing it was hopeless, Highgrade began turning his pockets out, searching for loose coins.

The stranger sighed.

"Maybe we can do a deal," he said.

Lights glinted in the depths of Highgrade's filmy eyes.

"Now you're talking!" he said.

"Watering these mules is a chore. Finish it for me and you can have a drink. You won't even have to do the whole team because I've already tended to a couple of them."

"It's a go," Highgrade said.

The stranger handed him the bucket. Highgrade staggered down to the creek. He slipped on the muddy bank and stepped into the water up to his ankles. It was cold.

He filled the bucket and started back, eyes small and hot, breath wheezing. Water slopped over the rim with every step. When he reached the wagon, half the water was gone.

The stranger said, "What the hell?"

"Sorry, mister, I'm a little shaky. If I just had a little nip to steady my nerves, I'd be fine."

"I doubt it," the stranger said. "That's what I get for not minding my own business," he said.

Reaching under the front seat of the wagon, he hauled out a half-gallon brown jug. Tied to the neck handle by a rawhide thong was a tin cup. Uncorking it, he poured out some pale brown fluid into the cup, filling it halfway.

He held the jug tightly, as if suspecting that the other planned to make a grab for it. The tin cup was on a long leash. He handed it to Highgrade.

"Here."

"Thanks, mister, thanks. You don't know—"

"I do know. I've been there myself. Shut up and drink."

Highgrade held the cup in both hands. The fumes made his nose burn and his eyes tear. He drank slowly, carefully, not spilling a single drop.

His parched mouth soaked it up like a sponge. It burned going down his throat, kindling a fire in his belly. His quavery, hollow feeling went away, replaced by a sense of well-grounded solidity. The cylinders of his brain unfroze and began to work. The hammering sound persisted, but he shrugged it off.

"Ah," he said.

The empty cup was plucked from his hands and tucked away with the brown jug in the wagon's boot.

Highgrade looked at the stranger and saw him for the first time since the encounter began.

"I know you. You're the man who killed the town of Blue Meadow," he said.

"You can't be that drunk yet, not on that little bit," Slocum said.

"Drunk? That wasn't even enough to make me sober. But now I remember where I saw you last. You shot that fellow in the street, the one with the gold!"

"That's right. Of course, I didn't know he had gold when I shot him. But the gold seekers seem to have done all right without him."

"Depends on what you mean by 'all right,'" Highgrade said.

"They've struck gold."

"Sure. They managed to backtrack the dead man's trail up into the hills, to the Kettle. They found gold there, too; placer deposits and even some pockets of gold-bearing ore. But nobody's found the mother lode, the vein where the gold-rich rock samples came from. Or, if they have, the news ain't reached here yet."

"Good. That'll keep the pilgrims coming," Slocum said.

"Mister, they are coming. And they'll keep on coming until the last claim is filed on the last piece of dirt in the most godforsaken corner of the Kettle," Highgrade said.

His hungry eyes feasted on the sight of the whiskey wagon. "But you've already struck gold, mister. Liquid gold," he said.

"Yah. It's not doing those thirsty miners any good down here. So, if you'll commence to watering my mules, I'll be on my way," Slocum said.

Highgrade took the bucket and went to work, fetching water from the creek until all the animals in the team had drunk their fill.

"Bravo. I didn't think you had it in you," Slocum said.

"There's still some life left in those old bones yet," Highgrade said.

Slocum took his kit from under the wagon seat. In it there was food. He broke off part of a loaf of crusty bread. His knife made a whispering sound as he drew it from the sheath stuck inside the top of his boot. A formidable weapon, its fifteen-inch blade was razor-sharp, mirror-bright, with the "Green River" maker's mark graved into it just below the hilt. He sliced off a hunk from a block of beef jerky. He offered the bread and jerky to Highgrade.

"Don't worry, you'll get your drink. You've earned it. But it wouldn't hurt to get some grub into your belly first," he said.

Rumbling in Highgrade's stomach reminded him that he hadn't eaten for some time. He took the food.

"Why . . . thanks, mister," he said.

"De nada."

Highgrade wolfed down the food. A tin cup brimful of whiskey from the brown jug awaited him when he had finished eating. He looked longingly as Slocum stowed away the jug. He drank slowly, throat working, not spilling a drop. When the cup was drained, he stuck his fingers to it, swirling them around to catch the residue clinging to the inside, then sucked that off his fingers. Slocum took the cup, scouring it with a handful of loose dirt before putting it away.

Slocum moved along the line of the mule team, checking the traces, making adjustments where needed. Circling the wagon, he inspected the rigging. Highgrade stood beside it, breathing deeply, filling his lungs with the pungent fumes.

Slocum climbed up into the driver's seat.

"I'll be on my way. Much obliged," he said.

Highgrade scurried over, squinting up at him.

"Hold on a second there, will you, mister?"

Slocum's attitude expressed his eagerness to get going.

"Time's a-wasting," he said.

"Time is money, or so they say."

"They do say that."

Highgrade got a canny look. He rubbed his jaw.

"Suppose I could save you some time, mister. What then?"

"You're doing the supposing," Slocum said.

"That'd be worth money to you, right?"

"You're telling it."

"You did me a favor, now I'll do you one. Looky here," Highgrade said.

He pointed west, to the mountains. The saw-toothed top of the range was blurred by a steely haze that the morning sunlight failed to penetrate.

Highgrade said, "See that gray streak across the mountain-tops? That's the edge of a storm. It may be spring down here on the flat, but, mister, it's still winter up there. Now, unless I miss my guess, you aim to take this wagon up the Bearclaw Trail though Rodman Pass to the Kettle."

"You know a better way?"

"Happens I do. You might make it by the Bearclaw in dry weather, though you'd have the devil's own time doing it. But not if it snows, and, mister, it's gonna snow. Even a few inches of the white stuff will turn the upper reaches of the trail into a sheet of glass. That wagon'll slide off the edge to perdition."

"What do you suggest?"

"There's another way to the Kettle, longer, more round-about, but surer. Stick to it, and you'll get through to the top, snow and all. Take the Bearclaw, and that wagon of yours will join all the other wrecks lying at the bottom of the cliffs. And that sure would be a shame, to waste all that fine whiskey!"

"That other way you mentioned, that'd be through Firetree Gulch, eh?"

Unable to hide his disappointment, Highgrade was crest-fallen.

"You know this country," he said.

"No, not this part of the Front Range. But I did some asking around before setting out. I heard you could top the Bearclaw, even in snow," Slocum said.

"*You* could, maybe, if the bushwhackers didn't get you first. But not the wagon."

"Seems like you know this country pretty well."

"Like the back of my hand," Highgrade said.

He held out his hand to demonstrate. It was shaking, so he lowered it quickly.

"I could take you to the gulch, guide you clear through to the Kettle," he said.

"Reckon I could do that myself," Slocum said.

"You'll have your hands full. When the outlaws come after you—and, mister, they will come, the hills are crawling with them—you going to shoot and drive the wagon both?"

"It's been done, but having a extra pair of hands along might not be the worst thing in the world," Slocum said.

"You're damned right it wouldn't!"

"Got somebody in mind for the position, do you?"

"Yes—me," Highgrade said.

"I figured you were leading up to something like that. Well, I'm listening. Make your pitch."

"I know this country. What's more, I know gold. When you get to the Kettle—if you get there—miners'll be paying you with dust and nuggets. I know true gold from false. I can tell you what it's worth at a glance, when it'd take a so-called expert assayer like Bissell an hour's worth of tests to pass the verdict. The sharper ain't been born that can fool me about the yellow metal. I can tell you if a claim's good or worthless."

Slocum shook his head.

"I'm no prospector. I've seen enough gold rushes to know better," he said.

"Then you know the kind the rush attracts. Bushwhackers, backshooters, claim jumpers. Scum. They're already here and more on the way. You'll need someone to watch your back on the trail and in the Kettle, too."

"But who'll watch you?"

"I may be a drunk, but I'm no thief! Besides, who're you going to trust—a *teetotaler*?"

The scorn with which Highgrade invested the last word made Slocum grin.

"You've got something there, Highgrade. But this promises to be a rough grind. You up to it?"

"I'm in better shape than I look. Otherwise, I'd've dropped dead years ago. I'm a fool for hard work . . . so long as I'm fortified with my daily ration of rotgut."

"That's a problem. The miners'll pay top dollar for this redeye, but not if you go drinking up the profits . . . Still, I reckon that we might be able to work something out," Slocum said.

After a bit of dickering, they came to terms. Highgrade agreed to work for a share of the cargo.

"You get your share on delivery when we reach the Kettle. Once we get there, you can drink it or sell it, for all I care," Slocum said.

"Not including my daily ration," Highgrade said quickly.

"No. But if I catch you tapping into the kegs, I'll hang you up to dry, and that's a promise."

"Fair enough. It's a go. Let's shake on it."

They shook hands. Slocum's palm was dry, leathery, like the man himself.

"What say we have a drink on it?"

"You can have one when we reach Firetree Gulch," Slocum said.

"That's a long ways off."

"Then we'd best be moving."

Grunting mightily, Highgrade hauled himself into the seat beside Slocum. The mule on the left of the pair yoked nearest the wagon turned its head and looked over its shoulder, casting a cold eye on the newcomer.

Slocum let out the handbrake and gee-hawed the team into motion. The wagon lurched forward.

Slocum said, "What happened to the sheriff?"

"Vanished with the dead man's gold. Deputy Buck headed for the hills along with the rest of the whole blamed town."

"How come you stayed?"

"Pilgrims have been setting me up to free drinks in return for hearing all about the bonanza gold."

"There's no shortage of them, and more coming every minute."

"Sure, but the whiskey ran out. Then you came along. Providence, I call it," Highgrade said.

The jail was made of stone and was relatively intact. But the wooden frame buildings lining Main Street were mostly disassembled. What few structures remained were being taken apart by men prying off boards and pulling down beams.

"So that's what all that hammering is about? That's a relief. I thought I was hearing things," Highgrade said.

"Not much of a town left. Looks like a cornfield picked clean by locusts," Slocum said.

"Miners need wood, mister, for sluices and shoring up tunnels and whatnot. Ready-made lumber's a whole lot easier than chopping down trees and starting from scratch. Not cheaper, though, not by the time it gets to the Kettle," Highgrade said.

"If it gets there, you mean."

"Oh, it'll get there eventually. But the people selling it won't be the ones who hauled it up. They'll be dead, killed for their load by hijackers," Highgrade said.

"Pleasant thought," Slocum said.

"Wasn't theirs, anyhow. These are johnny-come-latelies. The real owners cleared out at the start of the rush."

Some of the men stopped working to stare at the wagon as it went by. Highgrade pulled his hat down over his face and slumped low. Somebody shouted, his words garbled by distance.

"Friends of yours, Highgrade?"

"No. Can't you go any faster?"

"What's your hurry?"

"Word might have gotten out that those gold-field maps I've been hawking to the tenderfeet ain't exactly genuine."

The wagon made it out of town without incident.

"You can sit up now, Highgrade. The coast is clear."

"Whew! That was a close one. I could use a—"

"Don't say it."

"Well, I won't deny that I'm glad to see the last of Blue Meadow, or what's left of it. Yessir, when you killed that varmint with the gold, you started a rush that killed this town just as dead, mister—say, what is your handle, anyhow?"

"Slocum."

5

The carriage stopped at a train station in the farmlands outside the city. The place was just a little whistlestop where the railroad crossed a farm road in a hollow framed by rolling hills.

Julian Roux opened the purple curtain and looked out the coach window. It was early morning, gray, before cockcrow. Mist was everywhere, breaking up, drifting past in ragged clouds. Fields were wet with dew. Somewhere in the woods atop the hill behind the back of the station, a dog barked.

The station was a white wooden box with a peaked roof. The windows were pale yellow smudges of light. The wooden plank platform was deserted.

"The end of the line," Julian said.

"A way station, perhaps," said the woman.

She sat opposite him. Her name was Belinda Gale—such was the name she gave, at any rate. She was young, slim, elegant. Black hair, gray eyes, tawny golden skin. Jutting cheekbones and slightly sunken cheeks gave her a lean and hungry look that was provocative and attractive, or so Julian found it. She wore a fur-lined gray cloak with the hood down, bunched in folds on her shoulders. Her dress was dark green with black braided trimmings. Brown kid gloves. Dark brown riding boots.

"Way station or not, it's a hell of a long way off from everywhere else," Julian said. "There's plenty of places to catch a train in town, too, you know."

"They might have been watched."

"Watched? Watched by whom, Mademoiselle Gale?"

"By the police, among others."

"Oh? Do you fear the police?"

"Not for myself, Mr. Roux. For you."

"Me? Why me?"

"You killed some men earlier tonight."

"In self-defense."

"The authorities might not agree. Sometimes they can be so tiresome."

"That's true enough," Julian said. "I don't mind putting a little distance between myself and San Francisco for now. That's why I agreed to come along on this long night ride to nowhere . . . the pleasure of your acquaintance notwithstanding."

"You're too gallant," she said.

"I can't tell if you're being sincere or sarcastic."

"What do you think?"

"I don't know. You're hard to read. You should play cards, you've got a good poker face."

"That must be a liability in your trade, gambler; being unable to read faces."

"I can read men's faces well enough. I think what I would do in their place and act accordingly. But no man can look at a woman's face and tell what's in her heart—at least, I can't."

"You didn't read Blackie Hawkins too well last night."

"Ouch! Well, Blackie knows his cards."

"I'm not trying to be insulting, Mr. Roux—"

"You're succeeding, despite yourself."

"I saw you shoot. Any man who can handle a gun the way you do has no business wasting his time in gambling halls."

"You'd be surprised. Some of our best killings take place in gambling halls."

"If it's kill or be killed you're after, at least it should pay well," Belinda Gale said.

Julian's eyes narrowed.

"That an offer, Miss Gale?"

"I'm not empowered to make offers, Mr. Roux. That's the province of my patron. My task is merely to arrange a meeting between you two."

"Your, ah, patron wants to hire my gun."

"You're free to make that assumption, if you choose. Or any other."

"Who is your patron? What's his name? Why's he being so cagey?"

"I've been retained as a confidential agent, so I could hardly reveal that information to you, Mr. Roux. Even if I knew it."

"You must know something."

"I know that a train will be arriving in a few minutes. You will board it, where you will meet with my employer in a private compartment. A business proposition will be presented to you. If you accept, you will continue on until you reach your destination, where you will be paid on completion of your services. Well paid, I may add—my employer is nothing if not generous."

"And if I refuse?"

"You will be asked to keep the details of the meeting confidential. You will be let off at the next stop down the line, fifty dollars richer, at the cost of nothing more than a few hours of your time. Not to mention being well outside the city limits with a good head start," she said.

Knocking sounded on the carriage roof, as the butt of a whip was pounded against it. Rising, Belinda Gale slid back the panel that covered the top hatch. Framed in the square hole was the driver's face, ruddy and glowering. He said something in a foreign language. The woman replied, in a few words of what sounded like that same language. The driver nodded, head bobbing out of sight. Belinda Gale closed the hatch.

"Russian?" Julian said.

"Yes, Dmitri is Russian."

"Where does he fit into this little ménage?"

"A servant, nothing more. Or less."

"Whose? Yours or your patron's?"

"The latter, Mr. Roux."

"Is that double-barreled blunderbuss part of his livery?"

"This is a dangerous part of the world, sir."

He shrugged his shoulders, trying to work the kinks out of them. The long night's journeying had left him stiff, sore, and cramped; that on top of the cuts and bruises sustained in the gunfight. Still, he had come out better than his opponents, a cheering thought.

He opened a door, stepping down from the coach into the gray damp morn.

"I shouldn't wander too far afield, Mr. Roux. The train will be here soon," Belinda Gale said.

Hooting sounded, muffled by distance.

"Ah, there it is now," she said.

It was still a long way off, too far away for Julian to see. Mist hemmed in the background, mist and shadows. Beyond the station, the rails curving back to the city became hazy in the middle ground before vanishing in the distance. Moisture clung to the depot's whitewashed walls. Dark trees dripped. A bird chirped.

Moving away from the coach, Julian looked up at the driver's perch. Dmitri sat there, silent, hunched into the depths of his greatcoat, pointedly looking elsewhere. Julian saw the other's hands, holding the reins. That meant they weren't holding the shotgun. Where was it? Not far, to be sure.

Julian paced back and forth, trying to walk off the stiffness of cramped limbs. Dmitri snuffed out the flames in the coach's twin sidelights. It was now light enough outside to see individual blades of grass.

More hoots, nearer, louder.

Rails hummed. The ground shivered. Motion parted the mist as a light floated into view, coming forth from out of the edge of darkness. A pale yellow disk, it hovered above the tracks, gliding toward the station.

Flat, coin-round, the yellow orb shed light without heat. A chaste pale moon, it rushed out of the west, out of the gloom veiling the Bay city at the continent's edge. In the east, grayness lightened into gray-blue. A rooster crowed, its squawkings more plaintive than the lonesomest train whistles ever heard.

Turning to see if Belinda Gale had dismounted from the coach or not, Julian was surprised to find her already standing

an arm's length behind him, to the side. He hadn't heard her
moving, and he was quick to detect such things. Her presence
was comforting, what with Dmitri at his back with a shotgun.
Dmitri was a total stranger with no earthly reason to do him
ill, at least none that Julian could think of, but all the same,
the hulking driver would be even less inclined to cut loose
with the scattergun while the woman stood within the line of
fire. Or would he?

Julian put such thoughts from his mind. If Dmitri wanted
to kill him, he could have made his play back at the square
in front of the Savoy. He hadn't spent half the night ferrying
Julian miles outside town just for the purpose of slaying him
at this obscure locale.

The yellow light resolved itself into a jewel in the crown
of the head of some great land crawler. Its long curved body
was thick, hard-edged, multisegmented; a giant mechanical
centipede scuttling across the landscape, thunder growling in
its wake.

A train. It rushed down the tracks, headlamp ablaze, black
plumes of smoking chuffing from the stack. Whistles tooting,
bells clanging, it slowed to a stop at the depot.

Steam wreathed the locomotive. Its inner workings clicked,
tapped, bumped, thudded; slow ponderous sounds, like heavy
clockwork machinery turning over. The engineer and fireman
in the cab were too busy to notice Belinda Gale and Julian as
they passed by.

Julian was aware of the weight of the guns hidden in his
clothing, a comforting feeling. He and the woman went side
by side down the platform, along the line of railroad cars. The
passenger cars were crowded, with every seat taken. A flatcar
near the caboose was covered with riders. They sat hunched
up with knees bent, taking up as little space as possible, the
maximum allowed to them by their fellows. Not a single
square foot of the floor remained open. It was bordered by
people sitting with their legs dangling over the sides. Some
sat close to the edge indeed. All sat out in the open, unshield-
ed from the elements. Soaked, sodden, slightly mildewed,
they were heaped up like bailed paper left too long in the
rain.

Julian said, "Quite a mob for an early morning jaunt. Where's everybody going?"

"Some word had to leak out, of course. That was to be expected. But I didn't think the news would spread this fast," Belinda Gale said. She was preoccupied, speaking more to herself than to him.

"What news?"

"I'm not at liberty to divulge that information, Mr. Roux. My employer will acquaint you with the facts—or not, depending."

"I'm anxious to meet this patron of yours."

"You won't have long to wait now."

A conductor climbed down off the train and went into a confabulation with the stationmaster, who had come out of the depot. Routine railroad business.

A shaky character disembarked, slinking across the platform. A burly farmhand returning from a big night in the city. His go-to-town best clothes were frayed at the edges. He was in worse shape. A young man, he shuffled along like an ancient, staring down at his feet, looking nowhere else. Bleak, bitter, broken.

He must have been a local, for the stationmaster nodded to him in recognition. His forlorn state must have impressed itself on the official, who began pretending not to know him, nor even notice him. Slogging across a wet field of knee-high weeds, he took the right branch of the dirt road, keeping to the middle of it as he went his weary way.

A man came out of the near end of a sleeping car and strode briskly toward the head of the train. A derby, loud checked suit, walking stick, and spats identified him as a member of what was obliquely referred to as "the sporting fraternity." His hair was pomaded, his mustached waxed. Flashy good looks, gone to seed. He frowned, muttering darkly to himself, ill-humored.

He was almost on top of Belinda Gale and Julian before noticing them. He broke stride. Seeing the woman first, he sneered. Seeing Julian, he scowled. Recovering his gait, he skirted the duo, going around the female, then continuing on his way. The pomade's sweet oily scent lingered.

An object bulging in his coat pocket—a gun, surely—flapped against his side as he quick-stepped. He put a hand over it, holding it to his hip, steadying it. Julian watched him carefully until he was out of pistol range.

He said, "Wasn't that Handsome Harry Nash?"

Belinda Gale gave him a sidelong glance. "You know him?" she said.

"I've seen him around. And you?" Julian asked.

"A trifling acquaintance."

"He didn't seem overly fond of you."

"He seemed even less fond of you, Mr. Roux."

"Yes. I wonder why?"

"The likes and dislikes of Mr. Nash are of no interest to me whatsoever."

She climbed the stairs that Nash had descended and started into the railcar. Julian paused at the threshold, looking back at the carriage where Nash spoke animatedly to Dmitri. Beyond, a watery orange-red wafer topped the slope, shining wanly. A few ragged cheers from the flatcar greeted the sunrise.

Julian entered the car. Warmth enveloped him. After a few breaths, the air felt close, thick. Sweat started from his forehead.

Belinda Gale was ahead of him, more than halfway down the corridor. Both sides of the aisle were lined with private compartments, the only sleeping facilities available on the rolling stock of this line.

Halting about two thirds of the way through, Belinda Gale knocked on the closed door of a compartment to her left. An interrogatory reply sounded from within. Julian was too far away to hear it or her response.

A conductor stuck his head into the far end of the passage.

"You two are the only ones who got on at this stop," he said. "You who we're waiting for?"

"Yes," Belinda Gale said.

"Then we don't have to wait no more."

The conductor ducked out of sight.

Belinda Gale stood to one side of the compartment door, facing Julian, beckoning for him to enter.

"Please go in, Mr. Roux. You're expected," she said.

• • •

"Moira Connell! You're the last person I expected to find here," Julian said.

"Disappointed?"

"Hardly. But you may be."

"I've never known you to disappoint a lady, Roux, except when the talk turns to wedding plans."

"That was never one of your failings, Moira."

"Lord, no! I'm the marrying kind, but you're not. Besides, I like my husbands old and rich. Less wear and tear on the merchandise that way."

"The merchandise looks as appealing as ever."

"I've still got what it takes, if I say so myself. But I don't have to. You just did," she said.

"You didn't go to all this trouble just to whisper sweet nothings in my ear."

"Not hardly. Take a load off and we'll talk."

Julian sat down in the high-backed padded bench chair opposite hers. The compartment was the best the line had to offer. The windows were closed against the chill dawn air. Outside, it was daylight, but the fringed tasseled shades were pulled down and a low light burned in a globe lamp mounted on a wall sconce.

Moira Connell was a full-bodied woman slightly past her prime, overripe, but no less provocative and desirable for that. She had taken pains to downplay her bold good looks. Masses of glossy, brandy-colored hair were primly coiled and pinned up at the top of her head. They were further hidden under a sensible traveling hat. Her clothes were stylish, expensive, wellcut, quietly tasteful. They covered but could not conceal the sensational physique contained within them.

The train started with a jerk, gaining speed as it rolled out of the station.

Julian said, "Where are we going?"

"You're going to the next stop down the line, unless you come in with me. Then you get to ride all the way," Moira said.

Julian lifted the curtain, peering out. Some commotion was

happening at the rear of the train. Some riders had been dislodged from the flatcar by the rough start. It didn't seem as though any had fallen between the cars, although it is doubtful whether the train would have slowed one iota if anyone had indeed gone under the wheels. The rest of the flatcar riders would no doubt shout the loudest in protest if the train did in fact stop for such a mishap.

Those who had fallen jumped up and chased after the train, which wasn't moving fast yet. But it was moving, and faster every second. Some on the flatcar held out helping hands to the runners, shouting encouragement; others jeered.

It was raw human drama but Julian was looking elsewhere, focused on the black carriage as it drew abreast. Nash sat in the driver's seat, holding the reins, glowering. Dmitri was nowhere in sight.

Julian glanced back at the tail of the train. All the runners had managed to scramble back aboard the flatcar in time—all but one, who had fallen. He crouched on all fours as the caboose slid away from him.

Julian let the shade fall. "What's Handsome Harry to you, Moira?"

"Laughs. He can be amusing, as long as you don't loan him any money."

"You've nothing to worry about on that score."

"Neither a borrower nor a lender be," she said.

"Harry didn't look very amused when he got off the train."

"He was insulted that I didn't take him into my confidence."

"A wise move."

"He can't sell me down the river with what he doesn't know."

"Neither can I, eh, Moira? But you've got to give me something to go on. How can I say if I'm in or out if I don't know what I'm in or out of?"

A shawl lay heaped on the seat cushion beside Moira. From within its folds she produced a flat silver flask, whose liquid contents gurgled merrily as she offered it to him.

A gun lay swaddled in the shawl, too; not a "ladies pistol," but a big-caliber revolver. Moira covered it with a fold, patting it in place.

"Harry forgot his manners when I gave him his walking papers. I had to remind him to act like a gentleman," she said.

Julian was silent.

"A lady's got to protect herself," she insisted.

"You don't need me for that. You're doing fine by yourself."

"You must be thirsty, Roux. Have a drink."

"What is it?"

"Brandy," she said.

Julian took the flask, uncapping it. The screwtop doubled as a shot glass. Passing the flask under his nose, he savored the spiritous aroma. He filled the cup near the brim, passing it to Moira.

"Down the hatch," she said.

Julian nodded. They tossed back their drinks. He drank from the flask. The cup ran out long before the flask, to Moira's displeasure.

Julian smacked his lips. Moira snatched back the flask.

"Too sweet," he said.

"That why you left me some?" Jiggling the flask, she estimated its remains. "A mouthful, anyway."

"I've had a long night, Moira."

"So I've heard."

"What have you heard?"

"You're quits with Blackie Hawkins," she said.

"That's right."

"You don't know how quits."

"Come again?"

"Never mind. How come you split with Blackie? You and he go way back."

"I got tired of being a Pallbearer. I was going to too many funerals."

"There'll be plenty of them tomorrow when they bury Clipper and his crew. Think they'll bury them at sea, Roux?"

"If they do, it'll be the farthest that Clipper's ever gotten away from dry land."

"Blackie sore about the split?" she asked.

"No. Why should he be?"

"Nobody likes to lose what's his," she said.

"Blackie doesn't own me."

"Good, then you can work for me."

"What's the game, Moira?"

"Look outside the door," Moira said.

"Pardon?"

"Look outside the door and see if anybody's there, please."

Shrugging, Julian got up and went to the door. He opened it a crack. Somebody stood there, on the other side.

Dmitri.

Julian opened the door wider. Dmitri stood in the passageway, legs spread wide, knees bent, balanced against the swayings of the train. A tiny pool of rainwater had collected in a crease in the brim of his battered hat. Arched black brows, inverted Vs; down-turned mustache. Coal-black eyes—hard coal. Big hands hung down at his sides, open, empty.

"Dmitri's all right. He's with me," Moira said.

"I'm not surprised," Julian said.

She frowned. "What's that supposed to mean?"

"You're too smart to leave yourself alone without a protector."

"Oh. I thought you were making some sort of nasty crack or something."

"That's because you're an evil-minded woman, Moira."

She did not seem to resent his remark.

"Ain't that the truth?" she said.

"Well, what now?"

"Close it, Roux. I've seen what I wanted to see. Carry on, Dmitri," she said over the gambler's shoulder.

Dmitri made a little head bow. Julian closed the door, latched it, sat down.

"I'll bet he's got that blunderbuss hidden somewhere under his coat."

"He'd better," Moira said.

"Friend of yours?"

"My slave."

Julian let that pass without comment.

"With him on guard, we're safe from eavesdroppers," she said.

"And Miss Gale? Is she with you, too?"

Moira laughed.

"That sounded like a crack, Roux, but I'll let it pass. Sure, I was a madame, and a whore, too, and plenty more, besides. Whatever I did, I was the best. Now, I'm rich, thanks to a couple of old geezers who had the good sense to drop dead and leave their money to me, their legal wedded spouse. But I'll tell you this, Roux: They died smiling."

"I believe it. But where do I fit in?"

"There's rich and there's rich. I've got just enough now to appreciate how it would be to be really rich."

"You don't have to sell me. I'm greedy, too."

"I trust you, Roux. Give me your word that you won't spill what I'm going to tell you."

Julian stifled a yawn.

"If you want to tell me, tell me. If you don't, don't," he said.

"I'll tell you. I trust you. You won't talk."

"Are you trying to convince me or yourself, Moira?"

She took a deep breath, let half of it out. Her hands were fists resting on the tops of her thighs. Her inner struggle as outwardly displayed amused Julian, who was careful not to show it.

"Getting information out of you is like pulling teeth," he said.

"Did you ever hear of the Kettle?"

"The Kettle? Doesn't ring a bell," he said. "Is it a saloon? Café?"

"No, no! It's a place in Colorado. In the Rockies, a high mountain valley. It's shaped like a bowl, that's how it got its name."

"Why didn't they call it Bowl?"

"How the hell should I know? Maybe the founders didn't think the name was ree-fined enough. Who cares what they call it! The fact is, there's gold there!"

"Ah, I begin to understand. *Gold.*"

"It's big, Roux. A bonanza! Fortunes waiting to be made!"

Her eyes glittered. Her voice was throaty, husky.

"They've struck gold in the Kettle," Julian began.

"Yes."

"Which is where this train's headed."

"Almost. There's no direct line to the Kettle yet. We can get there almost all of the way by rail. After that, we go by coach or wagon—or horseback, if need be."

"That explains why the train is so crowded. Everybody on board's got the same idea as you, Moira: to get to the gold first."

"I've got a few ideas they don't have."

"Of that I'm sure!"

"Call this crowded, Roux? This is nothing. The rush hasn't even started yet. The bunch on this train is just the insiders who got advance word of the strike, like I did. The news will be out in this morning's papers. Before the day is over, hundreds, thousands will be setting out for Colorado, just from San Francisco alone. But we'll be ahead of them."

"That's like being the first of the herd to stampede off a cliff. Gold hunting's a fool's game."

"Don't you think I know that, as much time as I've spent in mining camps and boom towns! Give me credit for a few brains!"

"Sorry, Moira. I don't mean to imply you're a fool. I know you wouldn't set out on a trek like this without some sort of a plan. Whether it'll work or not is the question."

Moira's green eyes were hard, bright, intense.

"I've got something better than a plan," she said.

"What?"

"Title to some of the most prime pieces of real estate in the Kettle!"

"I'm listening," Julian said.

He was still listening when the train passed the next stop.

6

Slocum and Highgrade were just out of sight of the Forks when they saw the dead man. He lay in a ditch by the side of the road, wearing only a pair of long johns.

Slocum halted the team. He gave the reins to Highgrade and got his rifle from behind the seat. The mules were restive from the smell of death. Highgrade had his hands full holding them in check.

"Poor fellow's been stripped to his skivvies," he said.

Slocum looked everywhere but at the corpse.

"What are you looking for, Slocum?"

"The killers."

"You reckon they're around?"

"Why not?"

The Forks was where the road south from Blue Meadow met the start of the Bearclaw Trail. Bypassing the junction, the whiskey wagon had continued along the south road toward the crossing at Big Elk Creek, gateway to Firetree Gulch. No sooner had the settlement at the Forks vanished behind the curve of the earth than the dead man appeared.

The road lay atop a natural bench between the prairie and the foothills of the Front Range. A strip of land stretching north-south cut by ridges and hollows running mostly east-west. Slocum searched the landscape. Shadows slid across it; cloud shadows, that was all.

"See anything, Slocum?"

"No. I'm going to take a look at the body. You stay here."

Slocum climbed down from the wagon, Winchester in hand. He approached the body by a roundabout way, studying the ground. At one point, he hunkered down so as to more closely examine a piece of turf. Rising, thoughtful, he went to the dead man.

The corpse lay slumped facedown in the shallow ditch, its skin as white as exposed roots. Toeing it, Slocum flipped it over on its back, so that it lay faceup. Brown muddy water from the bottom of the trough clung to its visage.

Slocum got back up on the wagon. He sat with his rifle across his knees.

"You drive for a while, Highgrade. I want to keep my hands free."

The team started up, the wagon lurching forward. As they passed the corpse, Highgrade craned for a look at its face.

"Don't know him," he said.

"Just another pilgrim. Sign tells the story, Highgrade. He was alone, riding north, probably to the Forks. Three riders came along the other way. One of them shot him from close up, killing him. Not long ago, either; the blood was still wet."

"But they're gone now, right?"

"Gone with his boots, his clothes, and his horse. Gone south."

"The way we're going."

"Yah."

The mules were eager to be away from the death site. Highgrade rubbed his face, kneading his cheeks, smacking his lips.

"That was ugly, Slocum. I need a bracer."

"Forget it."

"I'm not case-hardened like you. Seeing a dead man does something to me."

"If I have to give you a drink for every dead man along the way, I'll go broke."

Highgrade stared at him. "You think it'll be that bad?"

"Don't you?"

"I think I need a drink."

"Think what you please, but don't go reaching for that jug," Slocum said.

The wagon went over a low rise and down the other side. When it reached the bottom of the divide, Slocum pointed out a set of tracks that left the road, going west across damp grassy meadows before disappearing into a patch of bushy mounds.

"That's where our friends went," he said.

"Those tracks go in but they don't come out. Reckon they're still in there?"

"No, they're out. Here they come now."

Three riders came out of the brush, about seventy-five yards away. One of them trailed a riderless horse behind his own on a length of rope. They came on, their mounts moving at a walk.

Highgrade said, "Is that them?"

"I'd say so."

"You sure?"

"Keep going and see what they do," Slocum said.

The wagon started up the opposite slope. The riders altered their course, cutting a diagonal that would intercept the wagon well below the crest.

"They're still coming. Faster, too," Highgrade said.

He started to urge the team to greater speed but Slocum stopped him.

"We can't outrun 'em," he said.

"What do we do, Slocum?"

"Stop the wagon."

"What?"

"Stop the wagon."

Highgrade reined the wagon to a halt. About fifty yards away, the three riders came on at a trot. Slocum jumped down to the ground and fired a shot in the air.

"That's close enough!" he said.

The riders halted, reining in hard. One of the mounts upreared but its rider managed to stay on. Another man shucked his rifle from its saddle scabbard. Before he could raise it, Slocum shot him. He fell off his horse, not moving.

The horse that first upreared did so again, tottering on its curved hind legs, forcing the rider to cling to its mane to keep from falling. He clubbed the beast between its ears with his fist, hammering its skull until it dropped to all fours.

His partner drew a gun and fired at Slocum. He didn't come close, not with a handgun at that distance.

The mule team leapt against the traces and the wagon hurtled forward, climbing the hill. Spinning wheels threw off globs of mud. Highgrade crouched forward, down low, cracking the reins, not looking back.

Slocum pointed the rifle at the man shooting the pistol and blew him out of the saddle.

The spooked horse circled, turning the last rider so that he faced Slocum in profile. Slocum's bullet knocked him sideways. Riderless horses scattered.

Mules' legs and spoked wheels were blurs of motion as the whiskey cart careened up the rise. Slocum threw a shot in its direction.

A bullet passed through the top of Highgrade's hat.

He halted the wagon fast.

Slocum walked up the hill, reaching him in a few minutes.

"Team got away from me when the shooting started, Slocum. Lucky I was able to get them under control."

"Lucky." Slocum climbed up on the seat.

"Say, you don't think I was trying to run out on you," Highgrade said.

"Why would you want to vamoose with a wagonload of whiskey?"

"The mules were spooked! I couldn't hold 'em back! All I could do was hang on tight!"

"Well, you can keep driving them right the way they were going. I aim to be at the crossing by noon," Slocum said.

Highgrade started the team into motion. Forward, upward.

"That was some shooting. You sure can handle a rifle."

"Glad you noticed, Highgrade."

"Ain't you going to check to make sure those fellows are dead?"

"They're dead," Slocum said.

"You're almighty sure of yourself."

"I know my business."

"Reckon you do, at that. That sure was something. Knocked those fellows down like a turkey shoot, *bing bing bing*."

Highgrade watched Slocum in the corner of his eyes.

"They killed that poor fellow in the ditch . . . didn't they?"

"Yes," Slocum said.

"Because it would be a terrible thing to kill the wrong men, a terrible, terrible thing."

"When I draw the line and a man crosses it, I kill him. Honest men have no business trailing strangers in country like this. If they do, they're buying trouble. But set your mind at ease, Highgrade. They had the dead man's horse. You could see a pair of boot tops sticking out of the saddlebag."

"I didn't see 'em."

"You were too busy looking for daylight," Slocum said.

The tilted wagon crested the rise, leveling off. Highgrade looked back, over his shoulder.

"Those horses belong to whoever finds them," Highgrade said.

"It won't be us. Can't spare the time to round them up."

"They'd bring money."

"Trouble, too, if anybody asked how we got them. Besides, those miners are counting on us. We don't want to keep them waiting, not when there's a prize of gold for the first to break the whiskey drought!"

"You have something there, sir. A toast to that agreeable sentiment!"

"No."

Highgrade sighed. He took off his hat, twirling it. Two holes were punched through the top of the crown: one going in, one coming out. Highgrade stuck his finger through them, wiggling it.

Slocum said, "Wonder how that happened?"

"I might have been killed!"

"You might have at that," Slocum said.

Moira said, "My first husband, the late Mr. Connell, was what you might call a financial speculator."

"That's not what the state senate investigating committee called him," Julian said.

"They never proved anything!"

"How could they, when the subject took his own life during the middle of the hearings?"

"That was thoughtful of him, to do away with himself in

a timely manner, sparing his wife and friends any further embarrassment," Moira said.

The train rushed through hilly California scenery bright with midmorning light. Moira sat beside the window, out of the path of direct sunlight, in soft gray shadows. Darker than the dimness was a smudge on her left cheek near the corner of her eye. Roughly the size of the nail on her little finger, it was shaped something like the spade in a deck of playing cards, or so it seemed to Julian. A casual glance would have taken it for a distinctive beauty mark that only added to the woman's glamour.

It was the mark of the lash, gotten years ago in a bullwhip duel with Spanish Betty in the streets of Bender, Kansas, a railhead shipping point for Texas cattle. A wide open town not big enough for two such hot-blooded divas. They went at it at high noon of a dusty day on the main drag, having it out with wicked bullwhacker's whips to the amazed delight of onlookers. The tip of Betty's whip had flicked Moira's face near the corner of her eye, brushing it. Moira went wild. Rushing the other, she clubbed Betty down with the knobbed pommel of a whip handle, then laid into her with the black-snake until her arm got tired. Betty hovered near death for days. Rising unpopularity caused Moira to decamp in a hurry. Betty lived, but her face was too badly scarred for her to turn a dollar whoring. She died that winter, freezing to death after collapsing drunk in an alley one icy night. A year later her brother and two cousins from Santa Fe tracked down Moira to Virginia City. The triangle-shaped mark on her cheek branded her as the person they sought. That was when Julian Roux had learned her story, told when she hired him to kill Spanish Betty's vengeful kin. He'd had a streak of bad luck lately and needed the money, such as it was. She knew that when she approached him at his customary table in the back of Reed Mallon's Bonanza Palace late one afternoon. No sooner had the bargain been made than the trio in question entered the saloon. It was bright outside and dark inside, so at first they didn't see their quarry huddled head-together over a table with the gambler. Before their eyes adjusted to the dark,

Julian was up, shooting them down.

He wound up spending most of the money on Moira. She was expensive but worth it. After the money ran out, she wouldn't give him the time of day, but he didn't hold it against her. Nothing personal, just the nature of the game.

That was long ago. They had both covered a lot of territory since then, in different directions. Now their paths had crossed once more, putting them on the same trajectory, hurtling toward the gold-rich Rockies.

Moira said, "The late Mr. Connell traded in lots of mining deals, so he had to know what he was doing to keep from being skinned. He knew about geology—that's the study of rocks."

"I know what it is, Moira."

"Good. Then maybe you've heard of the Hayden Expedition."

"They were looking for gold in Colorado back in '75."

"Right. Hayden thought that Pikes Peak was a volcano or something and that the whole basin thereabouts would be chockful of gold. Mr. Connell was with them. They never did find any gold. The mister went off to do some prospecting by himself. He liked the look of things in the high mountain parks west of Palmer Lake. He found traces of color in some of the side canyons, not much, just enough to make it seem worthwhile to search for their source. He was wealthy even then, so he bought pieces of land that looked most promising. Bought them outright, holding title to them. He meant to go back and develop his holdings, but something else more important always called him away. The bird in the hand, you know. Then he met me and decided that there were better things to do than making money."

"Like spending it," Julian said.

"I'm talking about what *he* liked to do, not what *I* liked to do. At any rate, his deeds and properties became mine after he—left us."

"This land's in the Kettle?"

"Yes."

"If he thought it was good, why didn't he develop it himself?"

"It was a crapshoot. He bought dozens of properties on speculation. He wouldn't trust anyone to work the diggings unless he was there to watch them himself, to make sure they didn't cheat him. I was perfectly happy in San Francisco, and not about to leave it for the discomforts of a mining camp in Colorado. And Mr. Connell was not about to leave me. So there we stayed."

"Why didn't you develop it when you inherited it?"

"It was one of many such properties willed to me. Each was potentially valuable—Mr. Connell must have thought so, or he would not have bought them. But which had the likeliest chance of success? I didn't know. Experts might be able to find out, but what's to stop them from trying to trim the poor widder lady? Besides, I had enough money."

"So what are you doing here?"

"I decided I want more."

"Don't we all."

"Yes, but I can get it. You can, too."

"How'd you get advance word of the strike, Moira?"

"I keep an eye on my investments and my ears open for any bits of information that might affect them . . . One of my gentlemen friends is an officer of the bank. He was quite cross at being called away from me to take care of some rush business. The bank's getting ready to move on the Kettle. Syndicates are being formed to buy up as much land as possible, in the hope of hitting paydirt. That takes money and the bank is making sure that it'll be there when needed. They use a secret code to send messages back and forth over the telegraph to their agents. That's why the news about the strike hasn't gone public yet. Most of the men on this train are probably in the hire of bank officers trying to steal a march on each other. Of course, my gentleman friend had no idea that I had any holdings in the Kettle, or he'd never have talked about it."

The road switched back and forth with hairpin curves to surmount the rising grade, snaking through a maze of rock buttresses and hogback ridges. Sunlight and shadow flickered in the compartment. There was something lulling in the swaying of the train and the rhythmic click-clack of iron wheels on steel rails.

Moira said, "I'm going to the Kettle to inspect my holdings and manage them personally. Even if there's not an ounce of gold in them there's still money to be made selling them to the speculators. I'm no fool. I know better than most what a rush is like, the kind of scum it attracts. Dmitri would die for me but he's no gunman. I need a gunman if I want to play with the big boys."

"Which is where I fit in," Julian said.

"Yes. It was lucky for me that you split with Blackie when you did. When I heard, I sent Belinda and Dmitri to fetch you. And it's lucky for you I did."

"Why?"

"Know a fellow by the name of Bill King?"

"Yes."

"He's dead."

That shook Julian, but not as much as Moira's next remark.

"They say you killed him. You're wanted for his murder. So it's a good thing I got you out of the city when I did."

"Murder!" Julian said.

He made a fist. He wanted to hit something, but he made his living with his hands. Enraged, he still thought of that. He unclenched the fist, sinking back in his seat. He laughed, unamused.

"Blackie's tightening the screws. No doubt the charges will be dropped as soon as I rejoin the gang," he said.

"What are you going to do?"

"I don't like to be pushed."

"Come to Colorado with me."

"You're pushing, too, Moira. I don't like running away, either."

"It's not like running away because you're scared. The Kettle won't be any picnic. Go back to San Francisco, and then what? You either give yourself up to the law or shoot it out with any police that try to arrest you. Maybe kill one. Blackie'll really own you then, after he squares that. Or you can cool off in the mountains for a few months and get paid for it. And maybe get rich—"

"Let's skip the maybes."

"All right. There's no maybe that you'll be going back."

"True."

"Go back in a couple of months, when they're not expecting you. That'll help. You'll need all you can get if you're going to buck Blackie."

"I just want to talk to him, to straighten things out."

"That's one chat I'd just as soon miss." She sighed. "Well, what's it to be, Julian? In or out?"

Julian stroked his chin. "There's sense in what you say. But even if I throw in, there's a rough road ahead."

"I take it that's a yes."

"We'll need supplies—food, clothes, camping gear, guns."

"We've got them and more. Horses, too."

Moira leaned forward, eyes alight. "I know how hard it is to get provisions when the rush is on. When you can get them, they cost you an arm and a leg. And I didn't intend to ride this train all the way to the Divide just to sit there on my ass just because there's no horses to be had!

"Damned right. There's plenty of guns and ammunition, too."

"What would you have done if I declined your offer?" he said.

"Paid you off for your time and gotten someone else. There's no shortage of men who wouldn't jump at the chance."

"I like to look before I leap."

"You didn't when you broke from Blackie," she said.

The train rushed on.

7

By midday Slocum and Highgrade were in sight of the crossing. Much nearer was a small temporary camp that had been pitched on the rise not far from the road. A pair of hobbled horses browsed on dry grass. A family was grouped around a wagon; a man, a woman, three children. The man held a shotgun pointed down. A gun was stuck in his belt. He looked stubborn, resolute, alert. The woman shooed the kids behind the wagon. They crouched, clutching wheel spokes, peering through them.

Highgrade held the reins. Slocum sat with the rifle across his lap.

"Howdy," Highgrade said.

The man nodded. "Don't go down there unless you can pay!" the man said.

"Pay? How's that, mister?" Highgrade said.

"Hold up, Highgrade. Let's hear what the man has to say," Slocum said.

"Some hard cases have set themselves up in business at the ford, collecting tolls. If you don't pay, you don't pass," the man said.

"Like hell!" Highgrade said.

"Fellow named Ellis runs the bunch. A real rough-looking crowd, too."

"Ellis?" Slocum said. "Not Deke Ellis?"

"Come to think of it, he did call himself Deacon, or some such," the man said.

His face hardened. "Friend of yours?"

"No," Slocum said. "And if that's the man I'm thinking of,

you did well to steer clear of him. He's a mean hombre."

The woman poked her head around a corner of the wagon. "They looked like cutthroats to me!" she said, shuddering.

"How many?" Slocum said.

The man thought.

"Five, counting Ellis. They've got the road blocked off. There was a couple more down by the stream, but I couldn't see how many. I didn't want any part of them. I skedaddled out of there fast, and damned glad for the chance to get away. They could see it wasn't worth robbing us. I'd have kept on but the horses were played out. They'd drop without rest. Soon as they're ready, we're pulling out and not stopping till we reach the Kettle," he said.

Highgrade said, "It's none of my business, mister, but I hope you ain't planning on taking the Bearclaw Trail."

"Why not?"

"You'll have a tough time getting up it with that wagon."

"What else can I do? It's the only route there within fifty miles, except by the ford, here, and I can't pay the freight. Even if I could, I wouldn't want those hyenas at my back."

"There's robbers back the way we came," Slocum said.

The woman gasped.

"My guess is that they're there to get anybody bypassing the ford."

"Ben, what'll we do?" she said.

"We'll think of something," the man said. He sounded like he didn't believe it.

Slocum said, "Why not sit tight for a while?"

Ben frowned, puzzled. "I don't get you, stranger."

"You never can tell, maybe that roadblock will open up."

"Not while Ellis and his gang are alive."

"Like I said." Slocum tipped his hat to the lady. "Good day, ma'am."

Highgrade started the team, the wagon advanced. The sun was high but the winds blowing down from the mountains were cold. A long slope eased down into a flat prairie. Meandering across the flat was the sun-silvered coils of Big Elk Creek. Thick woods grew along the east bank. The west bank was wooded clear through to the mountains, though trails honeycombed the foliage. Bishop's Ford was where the creek ran its broadest and shallowest.

The descent began. Slocum said, "Can you shoot?"

"I can hit a barn door with a load of buckshot at close range, maybe. 'Course, I might be able to do better with a couple of drinks in me to steady my hand . . ."

"No."

Highgrade squinted at him.

"What've you got in mind, Slocum?"

"I know Deke Ellis. Mean little buzzard. Anybody taking orders from him is sure to be the same."

"What's your plan?"

"Oh, we'll just go pass the time of day with Deacon."

"That's not much of a plan."

Slocum shrugged. He took a gunbelt and looped it over his left shoulder so the holstered gun hung butt-out under his arm. He already wore a gun on each hip. He threw an old dun-gray blanket over his shoulders, huddling in its folds.

"What are you going to do?" Highgrade said.

Slocum fired up a cigar, puffing on it.

"You could at least offer me one," Highgrade said.

"I'll sell you one."

"Hah! You know I've got no money."

"You can have it on credit, against your share of whiskey."

"You're a hard man, Slocum."

"I'm the boss and you're the hired man. I smoke the cigar and you do the work. That's the way of it."

Highgrade looked worried. "I should renegotiate my contract before we reach the ford. After that, it might be too late," he said.

They were about halfway down the slope.

"Tell you what, Highgrade. We'll swap. I'll hold the reins and you can handle Deke Ellis."

"Oh, no. That's your lookout, Mr. Boss."

Slocum puffed away. "Smells good," Highgrade said.

"I'll save you some at the end."

"You're all heart, Slocum," Highgrade said, shaking his head sadly.

The wagon leveled off on the flat, taking the fork of the road that led toward the crossing. Bushes sprang up alongside the path, then trees, thickening into stands of timber, lofty evergreens. Their sharp piney scent spiced the air.

The cigar was smoked down to the nub when Slocum offered it to Highgrade. Highgrade grunted, but took it. The path twisted and turned, following the contours of the earth, looping around blind corners screened by thickets. Setting aside his rifle, Slocum drew both side guns, holding them one in each hand under the blanket. Tight corners demanded close-in action with revolvers, not the long gun.

It was still, with trees blocking the wind. Branches groaned, knocked, rustled. Far-off liquid sounds from the unseen creek. The wagon rounded a curve. Not far away on the right side of the road was a clearing in the pines.

A man stepped into the road in front of the wagon, waving his arms, motioning for it to stop. A young man, desperate, dirty, road-weary. Clad in ill-fitting clothes, oversize hiking boots. No gun in evidence.

Highgrade hung fire, poised between reining in or running down the youth.

"Hold up, Highgrade."

Highgrade checked the team. The youth had dirty yellow hair, beard stubble, feverish eyes. He rushed toward the wagon.

"Easy," Slocum said.

The youth faltered, slowed. Perhaps he sensed what he could not see, Slocum's guns held ready under the blanket.

"What's the trouble, son?" Highgrade said.

"My partner—he's shot bad—I think he's dying!"

The youth pointed to the clearing, where a second man lay on the ground, beside a two-wheeled handcart.

"Go take a look, Highgrade," Slocum said.

Highgrade flashed him a dirty look, but Slocum was impervious. The youth had already started back toward his friend. Highgrade followed. Pine needles carpeted the ground. The wounded man lay on his back in the lee of a fallen tree, with a coat for a blanket and a stone for a pillow. His face was whiter than the scallop-shaped fungus clumped on the fallen log. He shivered, teeth clenched to keep from screaming.

Kneeling beside him, Highgrade reached for the coat draped across the victim's upper body. The other screamed.

The blond youth wrung his hands. "It's okay, Dan, he wants to help you."

"Ain't—nobody—can help me, Rufe."

Highgrade gripped the edges of the coat. Dan flinched, gasped. Highgrade folded it back, uncovering him. A fist-sized hole gaped raw and red in Dan's belly.

Highgrade kept his face steady, immobile. Dan watched him closely through slitted eyes.

"Hmmm," Highgrade said.

He draped the coat back over Dan, who groaned.

"Like I said, Rufe—I'm finished."

"Don't say that, pard!"

"What'd he have to shoot me for? I didn't have a gun! Oh, God!"

Highgrade hurried back to the wagon.

"You stay here, Dan, I'll be right back!" Rufe said.

"I ain't going nowhere, Rufe. I'm too busy dying."

Rufe raced after Highgrade.

"How bad?" Slocum said.

"Gutshot," Highgrade said.

"What happened, kid?"

"It was the one called Fitch. He did it. Down at the ford. Dan wouldn't pay the toll. Said they had no right to collect it, they were nothing but thieves, that's all. The headman said they'd kill him if he tried to cross without paying. When Dan went around the roadblock, Fitch shot him. Just drew and shot him, like swatting a fly. 'He's killed, Fitch,' one of them said. That's how I know his name. 'He's killed, Fitch.' 'No, he ain't,' Fitch said. Dan didn't have a gun. Me, neither. The headman told me to get him out of there, they didn't want to listen to him carrying on. I got him on the cart and brought him here. I thought they'd kill me, too," Luke said.

Dan shrieked.

"It's getting worse. What can I do?"

"The best thing you can do for him is put him out of his misery, kid," Highgrade said.

"No! I can't—you're loco!"

"You won't help your friend any by losing your head," Slocum said.

Rufe subsided into agonized frustration.

"Fitch wasn't even mad when he shot him. I wish I had a gun, I'd shoot him!"

A series of screams ripped loose from Dan.

"Better look after him," Slocum said.

"Deacon's the headman. That's what they called him, Deacon. Funny, I always thought a deacon was somebody in church or something. Deacon . . . He wasn't mad, neither. More like bored," Rufe said. He returned to Dan.

"Let's go," Slocum said.

Morose, resentful, the mules went into motion. The wagon left the clearing behind a bend in the road. Above the treetops sounded Dan's mortal cries. Another turn, and they were muffled, faint.

"You could pay the toll," Highgrade said.

"I didn't reckon on the expense of a helper. I've got to economize."

"You can't deny me a drink, not when it might be my last."

"You don't want a drink, Highgrade. Better to have an empty stomach, in case you get gutshot."

Highgrade nodded reflexively. "That makes sense," he began, before catching himself. "Yipes! What am I saying?"

"Whatever happens, don't let the team run wild. Keep 'em in check."

"Why? What're you going to do, Slocum?"

"Pay the toll."

"With what, lead?"

"Never you mind about that. Just hold tight to the reins."

The ground began to rise on both sides of the road.

Highgrade said, "Too bad about that young fellow. The one who got shot, I mean."

"Damned fool, bracing a gunman without a gun in his own hand!"

"Well, he was young."

"He won't get any older," Slocum said.

Another turn, and the road opened out, bringing Big Elk Creek into view. Sunlight glinted on the swift shallow water. A broad pebbly patch of ground tilted down to the water's edge. The way to the ford was blocked by a pair of hogshead barrels with a wagon tongue stretched across their tops.

The barrier was more symbolic than anything else. The real obstacle was the gang manning the barricade. A handful of hard-looking men straggled into place behind it when the wagon came into view. They were tough, trail-worn, dirty. Not a man of them was without at least one gun, nor walked without a swagger. Each was distinguished by some small touch of personal flamboyance: a snakeskin hatband, gunbelt studded with silver conchos, a fancy gun, a gold tooth.

Behind the barrier, off to one side of the road, was an unhitched wagon. The brake was set and stones had been wedged under the wheels to steady it in place. In the wagon bed was a high-backed armchair with a man sitting in it. Other pieces of furniture were scattered around the site, including a once-handsome old bureau, handcrafted from fine cherry-dark wood, which had been shot to pieces as a result of being used for target practice.

Opposite from the wagon, about a stone's throw away, was a grove that had been roped into serving as a homemade corral. In it were eight unsaddled horses. Between it and the water was a stone circle holding the ashes of a cold campfire.

Highgrade started to pull back the reins.

Slocum spoke from the corner of his mouth, voice pitched low for Highgrade's ears only.

"Get as close as you can. Makes my job easier," he said.

The mules stepped carefully on the stone-studded sandy ground. The stones were round, flat on both sides, water-polished, streaked. Wind feathered the surface of the creek, stirring the sun-glints into golden scales.

Highgrade halted the wagon when the barricade was only a few feet away from the lead team.

"From here on in, it's your play, Slocum," he said.

Deke Ellis, the Deacon, held court at the crossing at Bishop's Ford. He was a onetime snake-oil salesman turned robber and killer, the leader of a gang of robbers and killers. He dressed like the St. Louis drummer he once was, in a derby hat, checked suit and vest, houndstooth stickpin. He sat in the armchair in the wagon, a seat from which he could pass judgment like a magistrate at his bench, using a six-gun instead of a gavel. A meaty man, with brick-red hair and whiskery jowls, his well-fed belly slopped on the tops of his thighs. While seated, he wore his gun with the holster hanging at his crotch between spread legs, where he could get at it fastest.

He said, "Howdy!"

Highgrade nodded.

"The road's blocked," he said.

Slocum sat silent, head bowed so that his hat covered most of his face. To all outward appearance, he might have been napping or drunk.

Ellis said, "This here's a toll road, brother. If you want to pass, you've got to pay."

"How much?" Highgrade said.

"That depends on what you're hauling. There's a sliding scale with the fee based on the worth of your cargo. The higher the worth, the greater the fee. What could be fairer?"

"No toll at all," Highgrade said.

Some of the men snickered, but Ellis laughed out loud, as if delighted. "We won't argue that point, brother. It's not a subject for discussion."

"This was never a toll road before."

"Times change, brother. But it's still a free country. If you don't want to pay, you're free to go another way. Not that I'd advise it. There's some pretty desperate characters on the road. They'd just as soon shoot you and take all you've got."

"Well, I wouldn't want that."

"Sure, you wouldn't. Better to pay something and keep the rest than to lose all, with your life tossed into the bargain. It doesn't have to be money—you can pay in trade, with part of your load. A fair recompense for the risks we take in keeping the crossing safe and open for responsible travelers," Ellis said.

At his nod, one of the gang moved to the fore, a sly-eyed

individual in a navy-blue frock coat. A crude imitation of a sheriff's star, cut from a tin can, was stuck in his hatband as a badge of office. He wore two guns.

Ellis said, "My assistant, Constable Rhodes, will inspect your cargo so an accurate valuation can be arrived at."

"That I will," Rhodes said. He ducked under the wagon tongue barrier and came up on the other side.

Looking up, Slocum said, "Hey, Fitch!" He said it easy, friendly-like.

One of the gang said, "Fitch and Larrabee went scouting upriver, but they'll be back directly—"

"Shut up, Broyles. You've got more mouth than brains," Ellis said. "This one's a troublemaker, boys!"

Slocum opened up with both guns, shooting through the blanket. The first shot took Rhodes in the middle of the face. Slocum poured lead into the gang, gun blasts booming.

Four men behind the barricade spun and fell as slugs ripped through them. Highgrade had all he could do to keep the mule team from stampeding.

Still seated, Ellis threw his arms up into the air.

Muzzle flares caused the blanket to burst into flame where the guns touched it. Slocum shrugged it off, throwing it to the ground.

Ellis said, "I give up!"

"Don't think I want you to," Slocum said.

He sent a bullet crashing into the other's chest. Ellis flopped backward, taking the chair with him, overturning it. He tumbled head over heels, crashing to the ground, an inert lump.

Slocum hopped down from the wagon, covering the bodies sprawled behind the barricade. One was still moving, mortally wounded but alive, hands fluttering like turtle flippers. Another, motionless, coughed, then groaned.

Slocum fired twice. Stillness reigned among the fallen. A cloud of gunsmoke hovered above the center of the road.

Unsure of how many bullets were left, but knowing they were low, he holstered one gun, replacing it with the fully loaded revolver in his shoulder holster.

Two men on horseback rode out from behind a thicket on

this side of the creek. They were beyond pistol range but that didn't stop one of them from drawing and firing at Slocum. He didn't even come close. Slocum fired back, missing, but near enough to the target to sting them into flight. They wheeled their horses around and dug dirt.

"Highgrade! The rifle!"

Highgrade tossed the Winchester to Slocum, whose gun was already holstered, leaving his hands free. His palms smacked the rifle, battening on to it. Shouldering it, he pointed it at the fugitives, but they were already gone, safe behind the cover of an intervening ridge.

"Too bad I missed making a clean sweep of it. Fitch and his pard got away," Slocum said.

"Funny . . . Fitch practically caused the whole shooting match, and he gets away clean!"

"I didn't do it to avenge the kid back there; I did it because they would have tried to do for us sooner or later. Even if we'd paid, they'd have tried for us anyway, them or some of their backshooting pals. My guess is that they were in cahoots with the three back at the Forks, not to mention a few other bushwackers roaming the countryside. While he was collecting tolls, Deacon could size up the cargoes to see who was worth robbing later."

"Makes sense," Highgrade said.

"He worked a deal like that during the Black Hills rush," Slocum said.

He climbed to the top of a man-sized rock on the north side of the road, rifle in hand, scanning the surroundings.

"Fitch?" Highgrade said.

"Gone to ground. No stomach for a fight."

"I don't blame him. You sure made fast work of his associates!"

"They made it easy for me, bunching up like that."

"It was some shooting!"

"They were sweepings. The real hellbenders are up on the mountain, where the gold is. Where we're headed," Slocum said.

He got down off the rock, emptied the brass from his guns,

and reloaded. Highgrade reached behind the buckboard seat, hauling up the brown jug.

"I reckon I've earned this," Highgrade said.

"Sure have. One cup, anyhow—your midday ration," Slocum said.

Highgrade filled the tin cup to the brim and a hair beyond, so that the fluid swelled convex over the lip. Holding it in both hands, he rushed it to his mouth and poured it down without spilling a drop. Blessed warmth blossomed in his belly, radiating through him, setting his brain alight with tendrils of liquid fire.

"Ah."

Slocum corked the jug, putting it and the tin cup away.

Highgrade said, "If that don't beat all! I look Death in the eye and you begrudge me more than a single drink!"

"It's a working day," Slocum said.

Slocum turned out Ellis's pockets. A wad of paper money was too blood-soaked to be of any use; Slocum tossed it away. Another pocket yielded a leather pouch whose clinking contents had a pleasing heft. Inside was a fistful of gold coins. Highgrade came alongside while Slocum was counting them.

"How much, Slocum?"

"Close to two hundred dollars."

Slocum let the gold trickle out of his hand coin by coin into the pouch. He pulled tight the drawstring mouth, sealing it.

"Half's yours, Highgrade."

"Eh? What's that? Did I hear right?"

"Fair's fair. You ran the same risk as me, so you get half the spoils."

Highgrade clapped hands, rubbing them together.

"Now, you're talking! That's big of you, Slocum—big."

Highgrade's face fell when Slocum pocketed the pouch.

"You get your half when we unload the wagon at the Kettle," Slocum said.

"Thunderation! I should have known there was a catch to it!"

"There always is. If you had money now, you'd go off and drink it up, leaving me holding the bag. By paying you off at the mining camp, I know you'll see the job through. Besides, there's nothing for you to spend your money on between here and the Kettle."

"The only thing I want to spend money on is right there in that wagon! Don't worry about losing me, I'm sticking to you like glue!"

"That's what I'm counting on, Highgrade."

"Got things all figured out, don't you?"

A heavy gold chain dangled its glittering links in a loop protruding from Ellis's front pocket, but when Slocum fished it out, the fob chain was attached not to a timepiece as he had assumed but rather to a silver-gray furry paw.

"What the devil is that?" Highgrade said.

"A wolf's paw."

"What'd Ellis want that for?"

"Good luck charm, maybe."

"Didn't do him much good."

"The wolf neither," Slocum said.

He was minded to throw it away, but some obscure impulse, a wordless hunch, stayed his hand. He pocketed it.

He said, "Go relieve the others of any cash they've got. They don't need it."

"Kind of ghoulish, don't you think?"

"Half of what you find, you keep."

"I'll get on it right away."

"Take their guns, too. Guns are worth money."

Highgrade went to the center of the road, where the bodies lay. "Whew! You sure ain't much on taking prisoners, are you?"

"What would I do with them? Nursemaid 'em to the nearest law, some fifty miles away?"

"I ain't complaining, just making an observation."

"Try working instead."

"Ain't you going to help?"

"I did my bit—I killed them. Now, you do yours," Slocum said.

Highgrade set about his task of ransacking the corpses. First, he gathered up their money, dropping coins and bills into his hat. None had more than pocket change except for

"Constable" Rhodes. A nice fat billfold was tucked away in an inside breast pocket.

Highgrade crouched beside Rhodes, with his back to Slocum. He licked his lips. Maybe Slocum hadn't seen him find the dollars. Surreptitiously, the hand with the greenbacks in it crept toward his chest. If he could just slip the money safely inside his shirt, he could retrieve it later—

A click sounded behind him, the unmistakable sound of a gun being cocked. Highgrade tossed the billfold into the hat.

"Honesty is the best policy," Slocum said.

"Sure, sure . . . "

Highgrade brought the money in the hat to Slocum, who counted it in front of him. Rhodes had about a hundred and twenty-five dollars, while the others all together mustered only a little under seventy dollars. Slocum added the sum to the money pouch and tucked it away.

"Don't forget the guns," he said.

Highgrade got a burlap bag from the wagon and filled it to bulging with firearms, mostly six-guns, with a few rifles and a shotgun. By and large they were good guns, expensive, well kept, as befit the one indispensable tool of the trade of their careless, violent masters.

"Why the long face, Highgrade? Cheer up! When we get to the Kettle, you're going to have yourself a nice chunk of cash money."

"If I live to collect it. Which is no sure thing, tagging along with you."

"Stow those guns in the wagon and have something to eat."

"I'm not hungry."

"Eat anyway. I'm not going to have you playing out on me later 'cause all you've got filling your belly is hooch."

"Yeah, and damned little of it, too," Highgrade said.

They lunched on tinned beans, jerked beef, stale biscuits.

Highgrade said, "I need a drink to wash this slop down."

"There's the creek. Help yourself."

"Bah!"

They gobbled their food in less than five minutes. Slocum finished first. He went to Ellis and stood over him, studying him, unconsciously handling the wolf paw while deep in thought.

"I don't like the look on your face," Highgrade said. "What devilry are you cooking up now?"

"Out of all these rannies, Deacon's the only one with a respectable bounty posted on him. I sure hate to leave him here for somebody else to collect on."

"Why not bring him along?"

"You think you're joking, Highgrade, but there's something to what you say."

"Like hell! I'm not keeping company with a corpse for the rest of the trip!"

"Not all of him, just the head."

"What?"

"I could take the head, preserve it in a cask of spirits until I turn it in for the reward."

"That's criminal, wasting good whiskey like that!"

"Who said the rotgut we're hauling is good whiskey?"

"I don't want any part of it."

"Not even if I split the reward with you?"

"No."

"Well, maybe you're right, Highgrade. The whiskey it'd take to preserve it is probably worth more than the head anyhow."

Highgrade shuddered.

"I said you were a hard man, Slocum, but I was wrong. You're a blamed heathen!"

"Maybe so."

"What about the gang's horses? They're worth money on the flat or in the mountains, and you don't have to butcher anybody to collect."

"I thought about that. But we've barely got feed enough for the mules, no less a string of horses. Those ponies would starve above the timberline."

"Don't like to see animals suffer, do you, Slocum? Just people."

"Especially drunks. Still, it might not be a bad idea to bring a couple along. If we've got to run for it, horses are faster than mules."

Slocum cut two horses out of the remuda: a bay gelding for Highgrade, and a black and white stallion for himself. Gunfire, bloodshed, and death had left the animals shy, skittish. While Slocum gentled them, he told Highgrade to pick the two best saddles and load them in the wagon.

Slocum inspected the saddles before securing them to the wagon. "I don't like riding another man's leather, but I reckon these'll do."

"You mean I finally did something right, all by my lonesome? Guess I ain't a complete jackass at that."

"If you were, you'd be pulling the wagon instead of driving it," Slocum said.

He tied the horses' lead ropes to the back of the wagon.

Highgrade said, "What about the rest of the animals?"

"Leave 'em. Whoever finds 'em can have 'em. Somebody'll be along directly, now that the road is cleared."

Rummaging through the burlap sack, Slocum found a gun he liked. Leaving it holstered, he hung the gunbelt on the tip of a tree branch hanging over the road.

Highgrade said, "What's that for?"

"That kid Rufe's somewhere around here. Probably hiding in the bushes watching us. He'll need a gun. Maybe he'll cross trails with Fitch again."

Slocum climbed up on the buckboard seat beside Highgrade.

"I know," Highgrade said. "I'll drive and you shoot."

Slocum took a last look at the corpse-littered landscape.

"We're all paid up here. Let's go," he said.

8

An S-shaped crack opened in the mountains. Its mouth gaped
open in the south, as if poised to take a bite out of the valley
winding through the foothills a dozen miles or so west of the
crossing at Big Elk Creek. The canyon wound upward to the
north, snaking between the peaks, now vanishing behind a
stone buttress to reemerge into view several thousand feet
higher up. A curving stairway to the chain of high mountain
meadow parks nestled in the range a mile and a half above
sea level. One such park was the Kettle.

The whiskey wagon climbed that path, creeping along the
well-worn trail in the center of the canyon floor. The route progressively narrowed as it rose, until its upper reaches became a
thin whippy line wriggling between distant pinnacles. Brown
claylike dirt made a thin tough covering over the rocky floor.
A dry spell had left it hard-packed, allowing the mule team
to make good time.

The first leg of the trek was a broad, U-shaped trough that
leveled off before curving west around a cliff. By midafternoon
the wagon crested the top of the trough, about a third of the
way to the top.

A panoramic view presented itself to the south, a magnificent vista of mountains and valleys. In the clean cool air, the
scenery stood out with the detailed clarity of an engraving.
Steely blues and grays predominated among the mountains.
Dark blue-green belts of shaggy evergreens banded the lower
slopes. Silver rivers and turquoise lakes.

That lay behind. Ahead, the route sloped upward, ever
upward, as it looped miles to the west before switching back

toward the east. The sun was on the decline, grazing the western ramparts, spilling blue-purple shadows across the landscape. In the east, a ghostly three-quarter moon hung high, a chalky smudge on a sky-blue slate.

Slocum said, "Shake a leg, Highgrade. Time's a-wasting."

"A leg ain't what I'm shaking, Mr. Slocum, if you don't mind."

Highgrade stood off to one side, taking a road call. Finishing, he buttoned his fly and returned to the wagon.

"Don't ask for a hand up," Slocum said.

Highgrade wiped his moist fingers on his pants.

"That's what comes of your hurrying me," he said, clambering up into the seat. "Be dark afore long, Slocum."

"Still an hour or two of daylight left."

"You don't want to pitch camp after nightfall."

"I don't want to camp here. Too open. Let's roll."

"You're the boss," Highgrade said.

Taking up the reins, he put the team in motion. The mules resignedly strained against the traces, and the wagon advanced. The two horses trailing behind were high-stepping and spirited, but then they weren't pulling the load.

The southern vista vanished as the wagon rounded the cliff. Now, rock walls hemmed in the trail on both sides. Fans of loose dirt and stones flared out from the bases of the cliffs, encroaching on the canyon floor. Boulders studded the way, some as big as houses. Most were the size of a full-grown bull, or smaller. The wagon meandered around the obstacles, up the grade.

A bend in the trail put the sun behind a peak. As the wagon entered a lake of blue-gray shadow, the air became noticeably cooler.

Highgrade shivered. "Brrr! Talk about your 'Valley of the Shadow!'"

"Don't go quoting Scripture on me," Slocum said.

But it *was* colder. He put on a pair of fingerless gloves, wrist-length black leather gloves with the fingers cut off past the first knuckles. His life depended on continued dexterity. The gloves would keep his hands warm without too greatly impairing their cunning. An old trick that he had used before in cold country.

He rewrapped the blanket around himself serape style, leaving his arms free so he could get to his guns. He was armed as he had been at the crossing, with a gun at each hip and a third under his left arm. The rifle lay across his lap.

"There's more blankets in the back," he said.

"That ain't what I need to warm me," Highgrade said.

"No, but that's what you're getting."

Highgrade tried wrapping himself in a blanket but it kept falling off. He couldn't get the hang of it. Cutting a slit in the middle of it, he pulled it over his head and wore it like a poncho.

"Just to show you how big I am, I'm not going to charge you for that blanket you just ruined," Slocum said.

"Hope the expense don't break you," Highgrade grunted.

They rolled on, on and up. As the grade steepened, shadows darkened and the cold increased. Sunlight turned the tops of the eastern peaks golden. Chill winds blew. Highgrade's hat flew off, sailing into the path behind the wagon.

"Aw, t'hell with it," he said.

"No, get it. A man needs a hat," Slocum said.

His was tightly tied down on his head.

The wagon stopped. Highgrade got down and started off in pursuit of the hat, which by now was a few dozen yards away. He moved stiffly, sore in every part from the long bone-jarring ride. Stooped, crabbed, muttering, he scurried after the hat.

No sooner was he in reach of it than a capricious gust of wind whisked it away from him. It rolled on the edge of the brim like a wheel for another dozen yards without stopping.

When he reached it, the wind tugged at him again. He jumped on the hat with both feet to keep it from getting away from him. That didn't do the hat much good, but it stopped its flight. Picking it up, Highgrade punched it back into some kind of shape and jammed it on so tightly that it hurt his head.

"You ain't getting away from me again," he said.

His voice was thin, drowned by the hushed immensity engulfing him. For the first time, he took notice of his surroundings. Gray-black cliffs rose hundreds, thousands of feet high, pillars of the darkling sky. The scenery had that distinctive sharp-edged focus that comes with twilight, causing every stone and tree to stand out in precise detail. That's all there was, stones and trees. No people, no human habitations.

Blue sky was bleached to the neutral colorlessness that precedes the dark. Only the very tips of the mountain peaks were tinged with pale yellow light, and even as he watched, they were losing their luster, tarnished by the setting sun. The wind sighed, gusting into moans.

Highgrade felt dwarfed, a jot of life adrift on the rocky spine of the continent. Just as the fearful solitude began preying on his nerves, something meeped nearby.

Startled, Highgrade recoiled, losing his balance and nearly falling. The shrill whistling cry sounded again. It came from a marmot poking its head out of a hole in a jumbled scree rockpile.

"You dern near scared me to death, you blamed woodchuck," Highgrade said.

His voice sounded even thinner than before, stifled by the solemnity of the all-encompassing stone cathedral. The wagon seemed far away. What if it should go off without him, leaving him along with night falling fast? A frightening prospect.

The marmot's chitterings pursued him as he hurried toward the wagon. "The same to you, pard," he said to himself, not aloud, unwilling to spare a breath that could be used to speed him to his goal.

"That's the fastest I've ever seen you move," Slocum said when Highgrade reached the wagon.

Breathless, exhausted, weak-kneed, Highgrade clung to the side to keep from falling. Leaning over, Slocum grabbed him under the arm and hefted him up into the seat, a feat of strength that he made look easy.

"I'll drive for a while," Slocum said.

Highgrade bobbed his head gratefully, too winded to speak.

The wagon rolled, the trek resumed. Shadows deepened from purple-blue, to purple, to black. The moon changed from a flat wafer to a three-dimensional orb. The wagon reached the westernmost curve point of the canyon, curving east and up along the next bend of the trail.

Highgrade said, "I ain't been up in the hills for a long time. I forgot how almighty lonesome it is." His breath showed as frosty vapor. "Even you started to look good, Slocum."

"You're just lonesome for that load of redeye. Got your wind back yet?"

"Yep."

"Then you drive," Slocum said.

Highgrade took the reins. The canyon walls narrowed, crowding the trail. Rumbling wheels echoed off the cliffs. Shadows were blacker than black. The sky above was a star-dusted purple ribbon.

Slocum said, "How far to the gulch?"

"Damned if I know."

"You'd better know, Highgrade. You said you knew this country."

"I do. I mean, I did, once. But it's been a long time since I was up this way, and never in the dark."

"Try to remember."

"We must be pretty close. Another hour or two to go, maybe?"

"You asking me or telling me?"

"Well, both."

The rising moon lit the way, beaming silver rays into the defile. Narrowing still farther, the passage followed a wavy course whose abrupt twists and turns alternately plunged the wagon into milky moonlight and inky blackness.

Close to three hours passed before the cliffs curved away from each other, widening into an oval ravine whose sides bristled with weird skeletal spires. A generation ago, fire had devastated the thickly wooded slopes, turning a pine forest into a graveyard of burnt trees.

"Firetree Gulch," Highgrade said.

"Hallelujah," Slocum said.

Sheltered from the prevailing winds, the gulch was an island of stillness compared to the open stretches of the trail where icy winds wailed. Patches of snow nestled in hollows and crevices. In the years since the first, a secondary growth had sprung up, scrub brush and thornbushes now brittle and winter-brown. Dead trees upthrust through the tangle, tilted at odd angles.

The center floor of the gulch, where the trail was, was relatively clear and unblocked. The wagon went deeper into it.

Highgrade said, "Ain't you never going to stop?"

"When I find the right place to camp."

"You already passed up a couple good spots. By the time you find one to your liking, we'll be clean out of the gulch!"

"If I had my druthers, I'd keep on going nonstop to the Kettle, but the mules need rest."

"Thank God for that!"

A mile farther, a cleft in the rocks to the left of the trail looked promising. Slocum investigated, finding it to his liking.

The site was teardrop-shaped, with the narrow end at the entrance. Within the curved rock walls was space enough for animals, wagon, and men. A crevice between the cliff face and the northernmost of the two encircling arms was choked with splintered rocks that served as a giant's stairway to a ledge about twenty feet above the ground.

"This'll do," Slocum said.

"And not a minute too soon! I'm bone-weary and ready to collapse!"

"Not yet. We've got to unhitch the team, tend to the animals, get the wagon squared away, and make camp."

"I'm glad you said 'we,' not 'me.'"

"Of course, I'll be mostly supervising."

"I never doubted it," Highgrade said.

The train stopped—Julian awoke. After a day and half a night's travel by rail, he had grown so accustomed to moving that not moving jarred him into wakefulness. He was alone in his own private compartment, opposite and one door down from Moira's. The compartment directly opposite hers was occupied by Belinda Gale. Julian didn't know where Dmitri was going to sleep. Maybe he'd just stand guard in the passage all night.

Julian lay stretched lengthwise across the seat, booted feet atop an armrest. A coat served as a blanket. His hat was pulled down over his eyes.

He sat up, his left hand holding the hat in place so it wouldn't fall off. The coat fell down around his lap. The black snout of a gun poked out from under a fold of fabric. He'd been holding it in his right while sleeping. He slept facing the compartment door. If anybody rushed it, he'd come up shooting with no delay.

Sitting up, he set the gun aside, rubbing his face. The train was stopped but he felt like he was still moving, an odd sensation that added to an air of unreality, a dreamlike quality. He tried to look out the window but saw only a ghostly image of himself reflected in the black mirror of the glass. He smiled. The reflection leered back, a grinning death mask.

Julian shivered. Well, it was cold in the compartment. He pulled on his coat, straightened his hat, pocketed his pistol. He'd take a look outside, stretch his legs a bit.

Easing the door open a crack, he peered both ways into the corridor, satisfying himself that it was empty before stepping out into it. Where was Dmitri? Off duty, perhaps. The hour was late.

As he passed by Moira's compartment, he heard sounds of commotion from within. He paused to listen. Panting, groans, convulsive movements. Dmitri might or might not be off duty, but he was definitely servicing his mistress.

Julian went to the end of the passage, opened the door, stepped outside into the cold dark. It was like being immersed in ice water. It numbed him before he could feel the cold. Bracing, in small doses. His head cleared, clouds blown away.

A depot squatted at the junction of two sets of tracks on a great dark flat. The moon was high; the sky, clear. Stars were hard, bright jewels flung across the void. The land was darker than the sky. The depot was encompassed by black nullity. No other structure, no landmark bigger than a bush, broke the vacancy from horizon to horizon. The western rim was banded with a saw-toothed sable ribbon that was the Sierras. To the east, a crooked line that could be the Rockies banded the curve of the earth. In between them was nothing but the prairie and the depot at the two-track junction.

A train from the north had brought a private car that was now being transferred to the eastbound train. The idling locomotive's headlight was a blazing yellow orb. Lights showed through the windows of the private car. Trainmen with lanterns walked the tracks. The depot itself was dark.

An irate passenger in first class intercepted a conductor hurrying along the line.

"See here, my man, why've we stopped?"

The conductor pried the other's hand from his arm where he'd grabbed him.

"We're stopped on railroad business and I'm not 'your man,'" the conductor said.

The passenger sputtered his indignation. "This is an unscheduled stop!"

"Yeah? Well, complain to them," the conductor said, jerking his thumb to indicate whom he meant by "them."

They were a group of men surrounding the private car, protecting it. They were without lanterns, armed with rifles, shotguns, and sidearms. They were quiet, well ordered, deadly competent.

"Who's in the private car?" said Julian.

"Some high muckety-muck, I don't doubt," the conductor said. "Complain to him, mister! Heh heh! I'd like to see that! Those bully boys'd drop you before you get within a dozen yards of him!"

"By God, I'll write a letter to the president of this railroad!" the passenger said.

"Who said he could read?"

"Damned impertinence! I'll have your name, conductor!"

"Bo Peep."

"Don't trifle with me, my man! I'll have you know that— hey! Where are you going? Don't walk away when I'm talking, you—"

"I'd better get hopping or they might get mad," Bo Peep said. By "they" he meant the gunmen.

The passenger let him go without further dispute.

"Damned gall!" he said to the other's back. Bo Peep trudged back to the crossing, falling in with a knot of trainmen.

The private car was to be joined to the eastbound consist. First, the flatcar had to be uncoupled from the train. A voice of authority ordered the riders to dismount from the flatcar until the operation was completed. Few wanted to surrender their hard-won places only to fight the struggle once again when they reboarded, so they refused to move. The cadre guarding the private car stayed aloof from the dispute, leaving the trainmen to confront the riders. The crew decided to carry on as if the riders were not there. If they fell off and broke their fool necks during the transfer, it was their own damned fault.

The flatcar was uncoupled from the train and towed on to a siding. Its occupants were clamorous, mutinous. Crewmen felt reassured by guns tucked away in their clothing. But if it came to that, some of the riders would have guns, too. The private car was coupled to the rear of the eastbound train. The phalanx of armed men stood prominently placed between the private car and the flatcar siding. The rowdies were content to stay well distant of the line of hard-faced sentinels.

Time passed and still the flatcar had not been rejoined to the rest of the train. The rowdies grew more unruly, but came no closer to the guardians. More delay. A hurried conference developed between some crewmen and two figures who emerged from the near end of the private car. Gratuities changed hands. The meeting broke up; a brakeman and Bo Peep came hurrying to the fore. Bo Peep carried a satchel hugged to his chest. The top was open; Julian could see inside it. It was filled with wads of money.

The trainmen darted past. Bo Peep was stuffing a wad into his pocket. The brakeman shouted something at him, probably bawling for his share of the skim. The duo halted about halfway to the engine, where it was dark and no one could see them drag down something extra from the boodle in the bag.

They continued to the engine, where the satchel passed into the hands of the engineer and fireman. A moment later the whistle sounded *all aboard*. Scant seconds later, the train started forward.

Julian put out a hand, grabbing the rail to steady himself as the train lurched into motion. Shouts from the cars indicated that others had been surprised by the sudden departure. That was nothing compared to the roar that came up from the flatcar when its occupants realized that the train was pulling out without them.

Nearer, the irate passenger was thrown into new paroxysms as the train began chugging away from him. He stood stupefied, openmouthed, and might have stood that way forever if not for the bellowed rage of those abandoned at the siding. Stung, he raced alongside the train, which still had not yet attained much speed.

Julian extended a hand, helping the other up on to the boarding stair, to which he clung panting while the depot fell away. The train was moving much faster now.

The flatcar riders charged. The guardians fired a volley over their heads, bringing them to a halt. Shots popped, a ragged crackle as lines of fire stabbed between the combatants. The guards cut loose with repeating rifles, firing into the mob, wreaking havoc.

Shots and shouts pursued the train on its ever-quickening course.

"By God," the irate passenger said, "by God! Did you see it? Prodigies of slaughter, man, prodigies! Of course, we're better off without the riffraff, but damnation! I almost missed the train myself! A fine thing that'd be, left behind at the station in the midst of that whirlwind! Bound to be a damned sorry sight now, a damned sorry sight."

"Glad you made it," Julian said.

"I wouldn't have, if not for you! I owe you a debt of gratitude, Mr. . . . ?"

"Julian."

"I'm in your debt, Mr. Julian. You gave me a hand up when I needed it. I'm Clardy, Rollo Clardy."

"Pleased to meet you."

They shook hands. Clardy said, "What's your line, Mr. Julian?"

"Oh, this and that."

"I've dealt in it myself from time to time. Still, there's only one reason for being on this train, and we know what that is, eh?"

"I'm traveling for my health."

"That's a good one! Me, too! After all, what's healthier than *gold*?"

Julian shrugged. "It's cold on this platform. I believe I'll retire. Good night, Mr. Clardy."

"Huh? Oh, yes—good night, Mr. Julian. Thanks again. I'll buy you a drink sometime."

Julian went back inside, leaving Clardy out on the platform. His hands were stiff from the cold. He put them under his arms to warm them. The door to Moira's compartment opened and Dmitri stepped out, closing it behind him. His shirt hung outside of his pants, the open gray greatcoat swirled around him. He saw Julian, blinked. Julian nodded.

Dmitri edged past him, toward the door. The big man radiated body heat like a furnace. Scowling, he went out on the platform. That should give Clardy a start!

The door opposite Moira's opened a crack. Belinda Gale stood behind it, her face hidden but for a narrow center strip. When she saw Julian, she opened it wider.

"What's happening?" she said.

"It's happened. We picked up some new passengers and got rid of a lot of old ones," Julian said.

He told her what had happened in a few brief sentences, voice pitched low, intimate. He stood beside the door as he spoke. Her black hair was mostly pinned up but a few strands had come undone, softening the clean sculpted lines of her face. Her garment was unbuttoned at the neck; the hollow at the base of her throat and the top of her chest were tantalizingly visible.

"Whoever's in that private car must be rich and powerful," she said. "Who can it be?"

"We'll find out before this trip is done," Julian said. "There's something else I mean to find out, too."

"Oh?" she said. "What's that?"

"What you taste like."

She stepped back, opening the door.

"Find out," she said.

Julian stepped inside. The light in the globe lamp sconce burned low, glinting in the darks of her eyes. Her lips were parted; her chest rose and fell with slow breathing. Her gaze was sharp, direct, eager.

Closing the door, he looked back—and saw Moira peeking out from behind her door across the way, smirking with satisfaction. He locked the door, locking her out of his thoughts as well.

Belinda Gale stepped into his arms, which closed around her. She was strong, shapely, softly rounded where she should be. She smelled sweet, her mouth tasted like musk and honey. She moved, and where her flesh touched his, sparks were struck. Kissing openmouthed, tongues thrashing, teasing. He pressed her back, caressing the smooth supple curve of her spine down to the swelling tops of her buttocks. His hands closed on them, squeezing the cheeks through her dress, kneading them.

She leaned into him, grinding her crotch against his, stoking the fiery hard-on stuffed in his bulging trousers. He stood with his feet spread, knees bent, braced against the movements of the train. Breaking off the kiss, he nuzzled the tops of her breasts, confined by stiff unyielding cloth, except where the collar was open at the neck. One arm held her around the waist, freeing his other hand to fondle her breasts, pressing, squeezing them.

Her nipples were hard inside her blouse. He reached inside, tweaking, teasing them. She worked deftly at his crotch, opening the top of his pants, unbuttoning them, uncovering his hot hardness. It throbbed in her grasp. He held her hips, working her skirt up, rolling it and the white undershirt beneath it above her knees, over round thighs in black stockings, past the ivory flesh above the stocking tops . . .

They had to disengage to prepare for the final embrace. A few deft movements, and she had stepped out of her undergarments, glossy black bush contrasting to white thighs. He shrugged off his coat, the gun in the pocket thumping when it hit the seat cushion and again when it fell to the floor. His pants dropped around his knees. He sat bare-assed on the seat, his member jutting.

His hands wrapped around her hips, pulling her to him. Holding her skirt up at her waist, she straddled him, kneeling on the seat facing him. She crouched, her sex poised quivering over his upheld cock. His other hand held her waist. Her hands pressed his shoulders. His cock head rubbed her silky lips. She caught her breath, front teeth nibbling the lower lip—of her mouth, that is. He positioned himself in place and pulled her down on him. She gasped, then sighed as she sank down on the rod, penetrated, enveloping. They moved together rocking and swaying, riding to glory on the gold-field train . . .

9

"Ring around the moon," Highgrade said. "That means a storm's coming."

Slocum said, "Get a good night's sleep, because we move out at first light. I don't mean rise at first light, I mean all packed up and ready to roll."

"I figured as much."

They were encamped under the overhang at the end of the side branch, bedrolls near a fire burning in a ring of stones under the open sky. The inches-deep layer of powdered ash and cinder left from the firestorm long ago cushioned the hard ground. A faint sodden smell of burning overhung the gulch. Enough second growth and dead wood was at hand to supply kindling for the campfire. A pile of such foraged tinder lay heaped to one side.

Time passed. The fire burned low. Highgrade sat up, wide awake. Slocum lay on his back, wrapped to the neck in blankets, eyes closed, chest rising and falling. The edge of one hand curled out from under the covers, wrapped around the rifle that lay by his side.

Highgrade rose, stamping his feet and rubbing his hands. It was cold! Muttering, he trudged to the fire. He broke up dead twigs by the handful, dropping them on the glowing coals. Nurturing the flames, he slowly fed them ever-larger pieces of wood until a good hot fire was going. From squatting over the fire for so long, his front was warm and his back was cold.

Slocum slumbered on, unappreciative of Highgrade's labors. But as long as he was sleeping, what better time than to inventory the merchandise? Especially the brown jug cached behind the back of the seat . . .

Highgrade was about half way to the wagon when Slocum said, "I'd hate to try shooting your hat off in the dark, Highgrade. I might miss and hit your head."

"You've been awake the whole time, consarn you!"

"I'm a light sleeper, where my property is concerned."

"*Our* property. Or did you forget that I got a piece of the goods coming to me, bub?"

"Payable on delivery to the miners, and not before," Slocum said. "As per the terms of our little deal."

"Bah! You talk like a danged lawyer!"

"That's fighting words to some folks," Slocum said softly.

Highgrade swallowed hard. "Sorry. That was a mite harsh. Guess I got carried away."

"Go messing with the whiskey again and you'll get carried away, all right," Slocum said. "In a pine box."

Highgrade bunked down, wrapping himself in blankets.

"You tend the fire next time it burns down," he said.

"Go to sleep, Highgrade."

Highgrade's pride was stung. He was determined to stay awake until Slocum really fell asleep, fast asleep. Then he would make free with the contents of the brown jug to his heart's content. No ordinary man could withstand the drunkard's dedication to quenching his thirst . . . Telling himself such things, Highgrade fell asleep. The day's exertions had even overpowered his craving for drink.

Highgrade dreamed he was dead and in hell. The preachers were wrong. Hell wasn't hot, it was cold. Ice-cold. Black bone-chilling cold that frosted the very marrow.

He wasn't dreaming! He was awake, sitting up, fists clenched. His heart raced madly, as if to burst against his chest. He couldn't breathe!

The cold dark was broken by a pale orange smudge—the residual glow of the campfire, banked down nearly to extinction. The fire glow helped Highgrade orient himself. It was dark, darker than before. Not only was the fire guttering out, but the moon had vanished behind western peaks. A thin pillar of smoke rose from within the fire ring, rising high and unbroken in the stillness. Slocum's dark bulk lay curled on its side, facing the waning glow.

Highgrade shuddered. Bad dreams must have spooked him, though he couldn't remember having any. It wasn't the onset of delirium tremens, the drunkard's hallucinatory mania. He'd suffered them often enough to know the symptoms, and he wasn't having them now.

The horses. Ah, that's what must have waked him! The black and white stallion and the bay gelding they had appropriated at the crossing were restless, uneasy. Hobbled and haltered to prevent their escape, they pawed the ground, sidled, snorted, nickered. The mules seemed uneasy, too, but they were quieter, not calling attention to themselves with noise. Probably they were smarter than the horses.

"Something's got those nags riled up," Highgrade said to himself.

A mountain lion prowling nearby, maybe, or a bear. But this range had been hunted out long ago, before the Civil War, in the days of the mountain men and fur-trading empires.

Crouching on hands and knees, Highgrade peered into the darkness beyond the dying firelight. Burnt trees were spiky, skeletal growths, seemingly more mineral than vegetable. Their trunks were netted with a mass of thick tangled underbrush. Did something move beyond that underbrush?

Highgrade listened. Bare branches rustled in the wind. But there was no wind!—or was there? He wasn't sure. Glimpsing an outline of something skulking at the edge of visibility, he blinked—and it was gone.

I'm spooking myself, he thought.

But he didn't get up to investigate and he didn't go back to sleep. A whinny sounded in the distance, quickly silenced. The bay and the stallion turned their heads toward the source of the sound, ears pricked, nostrils flaring.

"So you heard it, too," Highgrade said, low-voiced.

Why should he be the only one losing sleep over it? Slocum was the gunfighter, let him worry about it. Trust him to be sound asleep at a time like this!

Crawling on all fours, Highgrade reached for the sleeper's

shoulder to shake him mightily awake. His hand closed on a bundle of blankets. Blankets that had been arranged in a semblance of human form under the bedroll, a crude counterfeit crowned by Slocum's hat. Under the hat, where the head would be, was a dirty shirt rolled into a ball.

Slocum was gone. So was the rifle.

Highgrade looked around. Slocum was nowhere to be seen. Opposite the camp, at the mouth of the side branch, motion flickered. Thinking it was Slocum, Highgrade opened his mouth to call out to him—and promptly snapped it shut when he saw two more figures bracketing the first. Three man-shaped shadows flitted at the edge of the light.

Head swiveling, eyes bulging, Highgrade peered into the dark corners of the camp, as if determined to spy out Slocum by sheer force of will! He had to be hiding somewhere near about. The ruse of planting a decoy in his bedroll proved that Slocum was up to some stratagem. Apprehending the approach of intruders, he had gone to cover, hiding until he had the drop on the night visitors. But there weren't many places to hide at the campsite at this end of the side branch, and Highgrade didn't see Slocum in any of them.

"Where is he? Just like him to get safely out of the line of fire and leave me staked out like a Judas goat," Highgrade said, muttering under his breath.

The three shadows became hard-edged outlines as they began cautiously nosing their way into the side branch. Had they seen Highgrade yet? He must act while he still could. If only he had a gun!

There were some in the wagon, among them a shotgun. Shotgun—even he could handle that. No aiming required, just point and shoot. Double-aught buck makes a real mess. Might down all three with one blast, if they were all bunched together.

The rightness of exterminating three perfect strangers troubled Highgrade not one whit. Anyone who'd sneak up on another's camp in this godforsaken country was up to no good. He only hoped he could get them before they got him.

He was halfway to the wagon when the intruders reached the edge of the camp. Highgrade kept going, hoisting himself to the seat, reaching over the back of it, groping for the shotgun. It was too dark for him to see the weapons. His fingers closed on a six-gun—was it loaded?

A shot cracked, a bullet whizzed past his head, smearing lead on the rocks behind him. Highgrade froze.

Three men faced him across the camp grounds; tough, hard-bitten men. One held a gun leveled on Highgrade, smoke curling from the barrel. The others' guns were still holstered.

The one with the drawn gun said, "Raise your hands and bring 'em up nice and empty, you old goat."

"Whyn't you just kill him, Zack?" another said.

"I like to know a fellow afore I kill him, Harris," Zack said.

"Just kill him," said the third, bored.

"Then who's going to do the dogwork?" Slocum said. "You? I reckon not. No, I reckon not."

He was nowhere to be seen, but his voice was loud and clear.

"Who said that? You see him, Sherm?"

"I don't see nobody, Harris—"

"Come out and show yourself!" Zack said. "Where you at, you yellow cur?"

"Up here," Slocum said.

He was on top of the ledge, down on one knee, rifle shouldered and pointing downward. Zack's eyes flicked up. Slocum shot him. The *splat!* of the bullet smacking flesh was almost as loud as the rifle report.

"Yellow cur, eh?" Slocum said. "Hands up, you two!"

Harris and Sherm reached instead. The Winchester cut them down.

"That's what I get for trying to take 'em alive," Slocum said.

"Going soft?" said Highgrade.

"I wanted to question them about the route ahead."

"I don't believe they'll be too forthcoming," Highgrade said.

Motion erupted outside the mouth of the side branch. A horse and rider broke cover from behind the bushes. The rider spurred the horse north. Slocum rose, standing upright for added height, swinging the rifle around.

Other horses started from a place of concealment, riderless, scattering. The lone rider's mount missed its footing on a patch of loose ground, toppling sideways. The rider jumped clear to keep from being pinned. The animal scrambled up on all fours, more scared than hurt. It ran. The rider rose to his knees, shouting. The fall must have winded him; his voice was thin, weak.

From his perch on the ledge Slocum had clear sight lines on the ground outside the side branch. The dismounted one struggled to his feet, staggering after the horse, who bolted from him.

Slocum fired, knocking down the man on foot. He crumpled into a dark blur of twisted limbs, sprawled over frozen ground glittering with hoarfrost.

The body lay still, unmoving. Slocum put another slug into it, just in case. Not even a twitch.

He sidestepped down the top of the tilted ledge, jumping off when he was four feet above the ground.

"Fourth man stayed back, holding their horses. Tried to make a break for it. Couldn't have that," he said.

He looked each of the dead men in the face. "I don't know them," he said. "Owlhoots, just plain owlhoots, that's all. Mountains are having a run of them lately."

"So are you," Highgrade said.

Slocum untethered the stallion and threw on a saddle. Mounting up, he sheathed the rifle in the scabbard and uncoiled a lariat strung to the side of the leather.

"What now?" Highgrade said.

"I want those horses!"

Gritty ash was kicked up by the stallion's hoofs as Slocum rode out of the side branch in pursuit of the horses. Highgrade watched him go with no small degree of satisfaction.

"Hah! Outsmarted yourself that time, you did, Mr. High and Mighty Slocum! While you're rounding up those ponies, I'll just avail myself of the little brown jug!"

Panting, eager, Highgrade felt around in the darkness where the jug had been when last he laid eyes on it. His hands quested throughout the space, feeling for the glazed ceramic crock, not finding it.

"Little brown jug, where are you?" he said.

The mirthful mask of his face fell, crumbling with bitter disappointment when he realized that the brown jug was nowhere to be had.

"Where is it?" he asked himself. "Where can it be?"

The answer came to him: Slocum! Slocum must have hidden the jug earlier, possibly back when he rigged up the dummy bedroll while Highgrade slept. Highgrade could have wept for the perfidy of it all.

"The devil, the cunning devil," he said.

He wasn't licked yet. Far from it. He had been looking at the problem through the wrong end of the telescope. Why bother with one stinking little brown jug, when there was a wagonful of whiskey right under his nose? All he had to do was punch in the top of a cask and swill away until the stuff was coming out of his ears! Yes, and teach Slocum a lesson in simple human charity at the same time!

On the other hand, he had three corpses virtually underfoot as hard evidence of Slocum's casual attitude toward the taking of human life.

"Not that they didn't have it coming, the skunks," he said. "Didn't get to know me no better after all, did you, Zack? How do you like being dead, huh?"

Not much, judging by his face.

"And you, Sherm! 'Just kill him,' you said, like swatting a fly. But you're the one who's killed, heh heh heh!"

The mood passed from Highgrade, taking with it the momentary recklessness that had caused him to consider breaching a cask. Fun was fun, but drunk or sober he had no intention of incurring Slocum's wrath over a sin of that magnitude. After all, Slocum hadn't even been mad at those three, no, four fellows he had just killed, except maybe at Zack, for that "yellow cur" remark. Maybe not even then. With Slocum it was hard to tell what he was really feeling. But tapping into a barrel was sure to gain his displeasure.

"Besides, that way some good whiskey is sure to be wasted, and that's plumb unconscionable!" he said to himself.

Slocum returned, towing a line of captured horses.

At sight of him, Highgrade's self-restraint vanished.

"Where's the jug?!" he cried.

"You looked, huh? Figured you would," Slocum said.

"You set me up as a stalking horse to get the drop on a clutch of killers, the least you can do is let me get drunk, you son of a—"

"Ah ah, don't bring Momma into this," Slocum said.

"I didn't know you had one."

"Don't be unkind, Highgrade. I can still see my poor old silver-haired mother, just the way she was when I set eyes on her for the last time. It was back at the end of the war, in Georgia, at our old family place. That little spread wasn't much, but it was home. It was worth less than nothing when Sherman's bummers got through picking it clean. I had to get out; the bluebellies were after me as an unreconstructed Rebel. I rode out one step ahead of Yankee troops, riding for my life. And there was Momma, standing in the doorway of our little tumble-down shack, bless her soul, calling after me: *'Son! Son! You still owe six months back rent!'*"

Highgrade said, "Where's the jug?"

10

Slocum was going through Sherm's pockets when he found a wolf's paw; a furry, taloned, bloodless relic.

"What you got there, another one of them things?" said Highgrade. "Wolf paws must be all the style with the outlaw set this year."

"None of the others had them, just Sherm. And Ellis, of all his bunch. Ellis was running his crowd. I don't know if Sherm was the brains of these boys, but he could have been. So maybe only the leaders carry wolf's paws."

"Reckon Sherm and Deacon was in cahoots?"

"Could be," Slocum said. "Ellis did his robbing all legallike down to the crossing. He could act as spotter, see who was hauling what and how much it was worth. Later, his men could rob and kill the travelers farther along the trail, far enough away from Ellis so it couldn't be hung on him. Or, he could send riders ahead to others of the gang who were already camped in the mountains, telling them that ripe pickings were on the way. A fast horse could outrace a wagon even if it had a pretty good start."

"And the wolf paws? Where do they fit in?"

"Recognition signals, so that the leaders of different groups would know each other without tipping to outsiders. Like a secret code or handshake. That means the gang is pretty damned big, so big that all of its members don't know each other."

"Then Deacon and Sherm were both part of some bigger outfit?"

"That's how I see it," Slocum said.

"Where does that leave us?"

"Closing on the Kettle with a storm on the way and outlaws all over the place."

Highgrade eyed the four corpses laid out faceup over to one side, as far opposite from the penned animals as they could get.

"You sure been opening some vacancies in the membership, Slocum. If them others find out, they're sure going to be mad at you!"

"Mad at *us*."

Highgrade's eyebrows lifted. "Why me? I didn't kill nobody, you did!"

"Doesn't matter. You're my associate, so you're in the soup with me."

"Associate? What's that, a fancy word for 'stooge'?"

"In your case, yes," Slocum said. "But the outlaws aren't going to find out, because I'm not going to tell them and neither are you."

"My lips are sealed," Highgrade said, "except where that salubrious redeye is concerned. Suppose you scare up that little brown jug, hmmm?"

"Break camp first."

"The hell you say! I ain't doing another lick of work until I get my nourishment," Highgrade said. "The way things are going, I could get killed any minute and I don't intend to die sober!"

Slocum, sighing, retrieved the jug, which had been hidden in a rocky crevice.

"So that's where you had it hidden, you sneaky so-and-so," Highgrade said.

The liquid contents gurgled merrily as Slocum set down the brown jug on the wagon's lowered tailgate. Highgrade smacked his lips, his eyes shining. The cork was drawn, a cup was poured and drunk. Highgrade shuddered, snorting, tears starting from his eyes.

"Good, huh?"

"No," Highgrade said, "but it works."

A stir rippled through the mules and horses. Noise sounded

outside the side branch, on the gulch floor. Hoofbeats, slow and measured.

"Company's coming," Slocum said.

"This time I'm ready for 'em!" Highgrade said.

He pulled back his coat, revealing a gun tucked into his waistband.

"After last night, I ain't going to be caught empty-handed again! From here on in, I'm packing iron!"

"Careful you don't do something stupid, Highgrade."

"Don't worry about me! I know what I'm doing."

"I'm not," Slocum said. "Drunks with guns make me nervous."

"Nobody's going to get drunk on the piddling little thimblefuls you dole out," Highgrade said.

Slocum moved off to one side, out of the direct line of fire from the side branch mouth. He crouched, rifle in hand. Highgrade sheltered behind a corner of the wagon.

It was the hour of the false dawn, the wan eastern light that precedes the sunrise. Grayness roofed the sky, overcast from horizon to horizon. A frosty morn, chill and bitter dampness were thick in the air.

A lone rider floated into view, climbing upslope from the south, outlined against the openness at the side branch's head. Spying the camp he halloed it, waving his hat in his hand as he hollered.

"Who's that?" Highgrade said.

"It's that kid from the ford," said Slocum.

"Who, Rube?"

"Rufe."

Highgrade shrugged. Slocum told Rufe to come on in. Highgrade grabbed the brown jug and darted behind the wagon.

"Aw, for Pete's sake," Slocum said.

Long-legged strides took him to the far side of the wagon, where Highgrade crouched, upending the jug. His chuggings sounded like floodwater gushing from a drain pipe. Slocum repossessed the jug, not gently. Highgrade sat down hard, face cherry-red, mouth and chin moist and gleaming.

He chortled. "Hee! Caught you napping that time, didn't I, Slocum?"

Slocum tsk-tsked. "You should be ashamed of yourself, Highgrade. You've just about killed this poor old jug."

From the sound of what remained swirling around in the bottom of the crock, it couldn't be much more than a mouthful.

"Here, you might as well finish it off. I'm sure not going to drink from it after you did."

"I ain't proud, Slocum. I'll take it." Which he did.

Slocum grabbed the other's arm, hefting him to his feet. He reached under Highgrade's coat and lifted his gun in an eye blink.

"Hey, what are you doing—?" Highgrade said.

"I told you I don't like drunks with guns," Slocum said. "And that booze you guzzled is coming out of your share."

"It was worth it!"

Rufe rode in, reining to a halt. He sat his mount like a farmboy straddling a plow horse. He was lean, gangly, and rawboned, with a low forehead and a lot of jaw and chin. Goggling at the corpses laid out in a row, he was half puzzled, half resentful, as if suspecting that the scene had been staged solely for the purpose of putting one over on him.

"More dead 'uns! What's going on here?" he said.

"Beats me," Slocum said. "That's how we found them. We just got here ourselves."

Rufe frowned, then guffawed. "Pshaw! You couldn't have just got here—you're breaking camp!"

"That's right. It's too crowded around here. Hop to it, Highgrade."

"Yes, sir!"

Highgrade gave Slocum an elaborate salute.

"Fun's fun, and you've had yours," Slocum said. "Don't make me light a fire under your ass to get a day's work out of you."

"Yes, sir! I mean, no, sir!"

Highgrade set about his chores with a show of diligence, of which there was more show than diligence.

Rufe shook his head, his face disgusted. "What do you keep that old drunk around for?"

"He doesn't ask a lot of fool questions," Slocum said, going about his business.

"No point in trying to shine me on, mister. I know who you are," Rufe said. "You're the one who cleaned up on Deacon's crowd!"

"Not me," Slocum said. "I'm just an honest tradesman who minds his own business. I'd advise you to do likewise."

Rufe edged his horse to the row of corpses.

"Ain't that a sight, all laid out like they was in a funeral parlor, haw haw haw!"

He was horse-faced and buck-toothed, with shaggy eyebrows and lank strands of hair sticking out from under his hat. He stared each of the dead men in the face.

"If you're looking for Fitch, he's not there," Slocum said.

"Fitch! What do you know about him?" Rufe said.

"He got away at the ford. That's the last I saw of him."

"Fitch! He won't get away from me. Someday I'll find him and kill him."

"Good for you," Slocum said.

"He sure did for old Dan, I reckon."

"You 'reckon'?"

Slocum looked at the other, who was oblivious to his scrutiny.

"I didn't stick around for the finish," Rufe said. "Ol' Dan was taking a long time dying, so I said so long and moved on."

"Left him to die alone, eh?"

Rufe shrugged. "Wasn't nothing I could do for him. He was gonna die anyway. Besides, he didn't even know I was there. He wasn't kin to me or nothing."

"Kid, you're not as dumb as you look," Slocum said. Rufe bristled but Slocum ignored it.

"I thought you were a piece of work, Highgrade, but the kid's got you beat all hollow," Slocum added.

Highgrade felt no pleasure at the backhanded compliment.

"Hah! Look who's talking," he said. "Who made you God, Slocum?"

"Sam Colt."

The mules were harnessed, hitched to the wagon. The black and the bay trailed on ropes behind the back of the wagon. The horses were saddled for a quick getaway. The wagon was ready to roll.

The dead men's hobbled horses were penned in a sidepocket in the rock walls. "What about them?" Rufe said.

"What about them?" said Slocum.

"You leaving them behind?"

"They're not mine. I don't want them."

Rufe smirked. "Can I have them?"

"If you don't mind explaining to friends of the owners how you happened to come by the horses."

"Shucks, I don't mind," Rufe said. "I'll tell them I got them from you."

He laughed like he thought it was funny, an obnoxious bray that made more than one mule pick up its ears. Slocum, about to climb up on the wagon seat, stepped down and faced Rufe on his horse. Rufe stopped laughing.

"I could save a lot of trouble by putting a bullet in you now," Slocum said.

Rufe raised his hands palms up, as if to push Slocum back.

"I was just funning," he said. "I didn't mean nothing by it, I was just making talk!"

"Now, I'll make some," Slocum said. "You're wearing a gun."

The gun that Slocum had left dangling from a tree on the right bank of Big Elk Creek.

"I ain't no gunfighter," Rufe began.

"I am," Slocum said. "Talk about me and I'll kill you."

"Don't worry, mister, I'll keep my trap shut!"

"No, you won't. You're a loudmouth. You've got that loudmouth look to you. You'll kick up a fuss first chance you get. Why don't I just shoot you now?"

"Why don't you?" Highgrade said.

"I ain't alone," Rufe blurted.

"Do tell," Slocum said.

"I got friends . . . know I'm here."

"Who? Answer quick, boy, don't stop to think up a lie!"

"Bunch of folks met at the ford once the way was clear!

We all crossed over together—safer that way!"

"What folks?"

"Miners, and such. Two peddlers. Gold hunters!"

"How many?"

"I don't know—"

"Yes, you do!"

"About thirty," Rufe said.

"Thirty."

"That's right, thirty, and I'm one of them! I rode ahead for a looksee and they're close behind."

"Yah? And what did you see, kid?"

"Not a blamed thing!"

"Tell it that way and you'll live to tell it again," Slocum said. "I'm tired of looking at you. Git!"

"You—you ain't gonna shoot me in the back?"

"You're not even worth shooting in the front," Slocum said.

Turning his back, Slocum climbed up on the wagon. Rufe studied that back long and lovingly. He was careful not to let Slocum catch him doing it.

"Ride out," Slocum said, "or go for your gun if you want to sing in the heavenly choir."

Rufe pointed his horse at the opposite end of the side branch and started it. Hairs on the back of his neck rose up as he passed under Slocum's level-eyed measuring gaze. He could feel those eyes on him all the way through the branch.

"There's a backshooter if ever I saw one," Highgrade said. "Now he's got a gun to shoot somebody in the back with, thanks to you."

"I admit I misjudged the lad," Slocum said. "He's not so dumb. He was riding the best horse in Deacon's remuda."

"The best of the ones you left, you mean," Highgrade said. "You culled the best for us."

"Any complaints?"

"Only that you didn't ventilate that mean-eyed little varmint. Mark my words, he's poison!"

"If I went around shooting folks just because they rubbed me the wrong way, I reckon I'd start a lot closer to home," Slocum said. "Anyhow, he might come in handy."

"How?"

"If he makes a pest of himself, we can run him through the pass and see if he draws fire."

Highgrade pulled at his face. "That pass worries me, Slocum. If outlaws are going to be forted up anywhere on the trail between here and the Kettle, it'll be there."

"We'll burn that bridge when we get to it," Slocum said.

The wagon lurched, shouldering forward, the walls of the side branch opening out.

Highgrade said, "With all the bushwhackers and cutthroats hereabouts, I feel naked without a gun. Give it back, Slocum."

"Maybe later."

"Now. I got a right to defend myself, Slocum. 'Lord helps those who help themselves.'"

"Not when they help themselves to my whiskey," Slocum said. "If there's trouble, you'll get the gun back."

"By then it'll be too late!"

"You going to handle those reins like you know what you're doing, or are you just going to let the mules overturn us?"

"Quit backbiting! I'm on top of the situation," Highgrade said.

The team arrowed out of the side branch, hoofs clip-clopping as they traded the ashy loam underfoot in the branch for the harder surfaces of the gulch proper. Wind had worn away patches down to the bare ground. Coming out of the branch, the wagon wheels slid on loose soil, slewing around the rear of the wagon. Panting and cursing, Highgrade wrestled it under control, but not before the wagon tilted up on two wheels. Hanging there precariously for a suspended heartbeat, it grudgingly planted all four wheels on solid ground.

Slocum said, "Give me the reins, Highgrade. You're not fit to drive."

"Take them and welcome to them!"

Slocum wrapped his hands around the reins. The rising sun smoldered dimly behind gray clouds. Chill winds blew. Highgrade grabbed his hat an instant before it could be snatched from his head. The mules, normally stoic in the face of hardship, which they accepted as natural law, brayed in protest at the first bite of that raw, bone-chilling wind.

"Storm for sure," Slocum said, "but when?"

Highgrade squawked, grabbing Slocum's shoulder and pointing downhill. Slocum had been so concerned with getting the wagon squared away on the grade that he'd neglected to notice much of the surrounding scenery, a lack he now remedied.

Massed at the south end of the gulch were a half-dozen wagons and thirty people. Rufe was about halfway to them. Looking back uphill, over his shoulder, he sneered at Slocum and Highgrade, then spat.

"Overgrowed sodbuster's brat," Highgrade said, "ain't got no couth a-tall!"

"Forget about him," Slocum said. "What do you make of the others?"

Highgrade peered downhill. "Pilgrims, looks like. Gold hunters. The kid told that part of it straight."

"They must be awfully damned dumb to use him as a scout."

"Maybe he's the only one wanted the job. What do we do about them?"

"I'd like to ignore them, but they won't go away. They're sure to gum things up, given half a chance," Slocum said. "We'd better palaver with 'em."

The gold-field express sped east, switchbacking through the western Rockies, racing to meet the sunrise. It was overcast on this side of the Continental Divide, too.

Julian Roux and Belinda Gale filed into the railroad dining car. It was early yet; only a few wan faces peopled the long gray gloom of the space. But the waiter was sharp-eyed, alert, punctilious. He took their order and went away, returning in due time with the food. It was lukewarm, not very good. The coffee wasn't good, either, but at least it was hot.

Belinda Gale didn't have much to say, which suited Julian fine. He didn't have much to say in the morning, either. On the rare occasions when he saw the dawn's early light, such as now, the experience usually found him stunned speech-less.

A figure entered by the door at the far end of the car. It was Blackie Hawkins. Somehow, Julian was not overly surprised to see him. Waving, Hawkins arrowed straight to him.

"Well, well, fancy meeting you here! Quite a coincidence, eh, Julian?"

"When did you get on board, Blackie?"

"Last night. You know that private car which joined the train at the junction? That was me."

Hawkins stood leaning forward with one hand on the back of Julian's chair and the other resting flat on the table. The onyx set in his golden thumb ring was the most concentrated point of blackness on the scene, harder and darker even than his eyes or the strand of hair curling down over his forehead.

He said, "Who's your friend, Julian?"

"Miss Gale, allow me to introduce Mr. Hawkins, universally known as Blackie," Julian said. "Blackie, meet Belinda Gale."

"My pleasure," Blackie said.

"Not necessarily," said Belinda Gale.

Blackie looked startled for an instant, then recovered with a grin.

"That's good," he said. "Aren't you going to ask me to sit down, Julian?"

"By all means. Make yourself at home. You will anyway."

"That Julian! Knows me better than I know myself," Blackie said.

Belinda Gale rose, saying, "Excuse me, I know you gentlemen will want to catch up on your reminiscences."

"Leaving so soon? What a pity," Blackie said. "Glad to know you, Belinda. Any friend of Julian's is a friend of mine."

"Really? Sounds incestuous," she said.

After she was gone, Hawkins sat opposite from Julian.

He said, "Trust you to find a woman on a train! And a

damned pretty one at that. Seems a cold one, though, Julian."

Julian shrugged.

"But then, that's the type of woman you like," Hawkins said. "Takes all kinds."

"You ought to know, Blackie."

"I do. So do you," Hawkins said. "What's she to Moira Connell? For that matter, what are you?"

Julian shook his head in admiration. "You get around, Blackie, I'll give you that."

"I hear things."

"Who from? Handsome Harry Nash?"

"That's between me and him."

"Maybe you heard who killed Bill King?"

"That, I had nothing to do with," Hawkins said. *"Nada."*

"Who did it?"

"Throw back in with me and I'll tell you."

"No, thanks. I didn't like the guy that much," Julian said. "What are you doing here, Blackie? Following me?"

"Talk sense. I like you, but not well enough to follow you to Colorado. You're not that good. No, what brings me here is what brings you here, I'll wager."

"And what's that?"

"Gold," Hawkins said.

Did the other solitary patrons of the dining car look up at the mention of the word "gold"? Julian was unsure. He decided to keep an eye on them, and two eyes on Hawkins.

Hawkins said, "Some rich men want to control the Kettle gold strike. They want it all. Hell, it makes sense. You need big money to make a go of gold mining today, especially in the Rockies. 'Least, that's what they tell me. I'm no expert on mining. I take my gold newly minted out of the pockets of men. But what they say stands to reason. Gold ore needs crushers, mills, separators. Expensive machinery and skilled workers to run it. Who's to pay for it? Not your small claim holders, with their little bits of land and their ornery ways. Only the combines can swing it. They're willing to spend money to make millions."

"How much did you cost, Blackie?"

"Trade secret. Throw in with me and I'll tell you," Hawkins said.

"No, thanks."

"Some of those miners are stubborn. They're so wrapped up in their dreams of striking it rich that they won't listen to reason. They can be awful hardheaded, sometimes."

"Which is where you come in."

"The combine hired me as a troubleshooter, Julian. If there's trouble, I shoot it."

"Am I trouble, Blackie?"

"Oh, I don't think it'll come to that," Hawkins said. "It doesn't have to, as long as nobody gets boxed in where there's only one way out. You haven't burned all your bridges yet, Julian."

"Give me time, I'm just starting."

"I would, but the others aren't so indulgent," said Hawkins.

"Others? What others?" Julian asked, knowing the answer.

"The boys and another half-dozen or so good guns. Thirteen in all. How's that for an omen?"

"Who's the Judas?"

"Any one of us, maybe all!"

"Maybe you."

"Me, most of all! I'll turn my coat quick as a wink if the price is right. What's your offer?"

"I'm just a hired man," Julian said. "You'll have to ask Moira."

"I know Moira. No doubt she could make me an interesting offer. She's made plenty of interesting offers in her day, and been taken up on more than a few of them, I'm sure. I'm not just talking about money, either. But speaking of money, you've got to ask yourself this: How can any one person, even a fairly well-to-do widow like Moira Connell, outbid a combine of the richest and most powerful men in San Francisco? How can she hope to beat a syndicate that can buy and sell her ten—twenty—fifty times over?"

"I give up," Julian said. "How?"

"If I knew, I wouldn't tell you, seeing as how we're sitting on different sides of the fence. But I don't know, because there is no way to beat the combine."

Julian glanced out the window at a stony slope bristling with treetop-tall black rock blocks. Ice patches silvered the rock faces. A thin dusting of snow powdered the hard ground.

"San Francisco is a long way off, and getting farther behind every minute," Julian said.

"Money has long arms, my friend. Look at me. Here I am already, with twelve more to back my play. The combine moves fast. They want the way cleared for their buying agent, so they rushed me along as an advance man. Hired a special express train to catch up with this one, so's I could be johnny-on-the-spot."

"Maybe you're on the Hellbound Train, Blackie, but at least you're riding in style."

"The private car, you mean? Belongs to one of those combine jaspers. He was only too glad to put it at my disposal. You should see it on the inside! Like a traveling hotel lobby, or something. Got its own private bar—a good one, too, mind you—and get this: It's even got its own private bartender!"

"No! They're treating you like one of the Big Four."

"Big Forty-four, you mean," Hawkins said. "But not only that, it's got its own private chef. Good thing, too. I can't stomach the slop they serve on these trains."

Glancing at the remains on Julian's breakfast plate, Hawkins looked up, smiling thinly.

"You must have a stronger stomach than me, Julian."

"Time will tell," Julian said.

Hawkins stood up. "Well, I've said my piece. There's no cause for quarrel between us yet. I won't throw down on you, Julian."

"That's big of you, old friend."

"No, when it comes to a showdown, it'll be you that's pushing it. I'm not going to start anything. Of course, what the boys do is mostly out of my hands. They're wondering why you're still alive."

"If they want to find out, I'll be glad to oblige them. Anytime."

"I believe you," Hawkins said. "That's why I don't get it. You're not yellow, you've still got your guts, you're not stupid. You know which way the wind's blowing. Why don't you get right before you get blown away?"

"I like to play against the house."

"Playing is one thing," Hawkins said, "winning is something else."

"I'm about due."

"Don't bet on it. See you later, Julian."

"I'm sure."

Hawkins turned, started away. After a few paces he stopped, looking back.

"It was that last job, wasn't it? The squatters on the tide flats . . . that's where you got a bellyful," he said.

"Not at all," Julian said.

"For what it's worth, I didn't like it, either. But so what?" Hawkins exited.

11

The convoy gathered at the gulch was made up largely of two groups, merchants and laborers. The merchants had something to sell and the laborers sold nothing but themselves. Both sides accepted Abner Orkus as their leader. He was the buying agent for a pool of small investors in Cañon City seeking to cash in on the Kettle boom. He'd brought cases of guns and ammo and outfitted his fellow travelers with them. Four or five men of similar ilk, but lesser, trailed in Orkus's wake; whether as followers or rival businessmen whose presence he tolerated, Slocum could not tell. Willoughby and Weems were itinerant peddlers hawking a line of cheap goods and catch-penny gew-gaws. Soapy Spellman and his wife, Sal, carted the makings of a laundry in their wagon—a lucrative trade in the mining camps. A group of would-be entrepreneurs had combined their meager wares in one shaky two-wheeled gig yoked to a crowbait horse. They mustered one extra horse between them. On the trail, one drove the wagon, two rode on the saddle horse, and the fourth and fifth men held on to the sides of the cart and jogged along with it. They frequently changed places to ensure that no one was cheated of his full measure of exhaustion. They looked glad for the rest at the stopover at dawn in Firetree Gulch.

Foremost of the representatives of the working class were four miners, Donovan, Farley, Hoy, and McBane. Five mechanics, pipe fitters, and carpenter's assistants from Palmer Lake formed another clique. They looked like they knew how to use the guns Orkus had given them. Unskilled but desperate to find work in the gold fields was John Hodge, the man whose wagon had been pulled off the road on the ridge overlooking Bishop's Ford. With him was his wife, Lavinia, "Vinny," and the two kids, Pete and Pearl. A handful of vagrants in even worse shape grouped around a rickety wagon and its gaunt, spavined team. It was a toss-up as to who would starve first, the horses or the men.

And there was Rufe.

Slocum and Orkus went off to one side to parley.

"No sense talking where everybody can hear," Slocum said.

"I quite agree," said Orkus.

He shooed away his human satellites, who seemed loath to leave him. He and Slocum went to a stand of evergreen trees.

"The wind's not so bad over here," Orkus said. He drew his coat tighter to himself. "Feels like snow."

"I'm in a hurry, so let's make it fast."

"You wanted to talk, Mr. Slocum. I'm listening."

"A lot of outlaws between here and the Kettle—in the Kettle, too. If we all stick together, it'll scare off attackers. They'll go looking for easier pickings."

Orkus looked at him expectantly, waiting for him to go on. He was sleek, well fed, prosperous, but hard beneath the layers of soft living. He wore a good gun and the gunbelt was seasoned and weathered, as if it had seen many years of use.

"So?" he said.

"So how about it?" Slocum said.

"I think not, Mr. Slocum. Your presence makes some of our party uneasy. With so many loaded guns and quick triggers . . . well, you understand. We have women and children among us. We must think of their safety and well-being."

"Two women and two kids," Slocum said. "I counted them. They looked okay to me. What's your pitch, mister?"

"No pitch, Mr. Slocum. I like to see others prosper. I envy no man his success," Orkus said.

"That's big of you," Slocum said. "By any chance, you wouldn't be dealing a line of redeye yourself, now would you?"

"Me? I'm flattered by the suggestion, but wet goods are outside my bailiwick. I daresay some of the vendors along might handle a keg or two, but nothing in the magnitude of your enterprise."

"Uh huh."

"Of course, if you were interested in selling a portion of your stock, I might be persuaded to take it off your hands, if the price was right—strictly as a speculative investment, you understand, so I couldn't offer you more than a very modest sum."

"I understand, all right," Slocum said.

"Of course, I can speak only for myself. Ask the others if you wish, but I very much doubt that any of them would care to accompany you. Nothing personal; it's just that they're businessmen, not gunfighters."

"Why should they catch a bullet when I can do it for them?"

"Well, there is that, too," Orkus said.

Slocum started back toward the wagon. Orkus had to walk fast to match his long, loping strides.

"I hope I haven't said anything to offend you," Orkus said.

"Not at all. Business is business."

"Exactly."

The whiskey wagon stood not far from Spellman's laundry wagon. The latter looked like a cracker on wheels. Long narrow slits in the tops of the long sides let in light and air. A sign painted on the side said, "Cheapest Wash in the West." Highgrade watched it from where he sat minding the whiskey wagon. Soapy Spellman was built like a butcher. He was mustached, dour. He wore a derby, long-sleeved striped shirt under a mouse-brown coat, baggy pants. His wife, Sal, was built wider than he was. She was more dour, too, but her mustache was smaller.

Strange sounds emerged from inside the laundry wagon: high-pitched pipings, shrill laughter, chatterings wordless as a babbling brook. Highgrade was reminded, not pleasantly, of some of the voices chorusing at the onset of an attack of the drunken horrors. But this was no product of alcoholic delirium . . . was it?

The laundry wagon rocked on its frame, jounced from within by its live cargo. Occasional thuds sounded when the walls were knocked. Highgrade looked around to see if anyone else had noticed the commotion, but the laundry wagon was set apart from the rest of the caravan, whose wagons, horses, and occupants were massed farther to one side. No sign of Soapy or his wife, either.

Highgrade climbed down from the wagon to investigate. He neared the laundry wagon gingerly, on tiptoes. He was close enough to the whiskey cart to run back to it if anyone tried to interfere with it. He just had to satisfy his curiosity about who—or what—was inside the laundry wagon.

The ventilation slits were too high up on the sides for him to see into while standing on the ground. He went around to the back of the wagon, where a tailboard served as a step to a blank padlocked door. A fresh outburst of gibberish commenced from within. Highgrade was taken aback by it. When it died away, he put his ear to the door and listened hard.

"Hey, get away from there!"

Highgrade jumped back, startled. He'd been so preoccupied with puzzling out the nature of the strange sounds that he'd been surprised by one of the owners, Sal Spellman, the laundryman's wife.

Sal was a two-fisted termagant, an ex-women's prison guard and former orderly at an asylum for the criminally insane.

"What for are you sneaking around back here?" she said.

"I ain't sneaking no ways no how, madame."

"Call me that again and I'll whomp you."

Under his nose, she waved a clublike fist.

Highgrade summoned up an air of offended dignity.

"Somebody was moaning in there so I came over to see if I could help. Sounded real bad off," he said. "Say, what you got locked in there, anyhow?"

Sal's eyes were sparkling slits, trapped in a web of laugh lines. She showed a wicked smile.

"So you want to know what's in there, do you?" she said.

"I was just trying to help out, be neighborly."

"Want a look inside, neighbor? Do you, eh? Know what I've got in there? Girls."

"Girls, huh?"

"Real live ones," Sal said. "Want a peek?"

"Not if it's going to cost me anything," Highgrade said.

He took a step back but Sal caught his forearm, her fingers sinking into his flesh, numbing it where they gripped.

"Don't be shy, neighbor," she cooed. "It's free."

Keeping hold of Highgrade's arm so he couldn't get away, Sal used her other hand to fish out a key on a chain around her neck. She used it to open the padlock. As she unlocked it, a new clamor erupted from within, accompanied by extraordinary vocalizations like the cackling of human chickens.

"Lord, woman, what kind of girls is that?" Highgrade cried.

"You'll like them," said Sal.

Soapy Spellman walked into view. "What's going on, Sal?"

"Neighbor here wants to see our pretties."

Soapy's grin got even nastier than hers.

"Haw! Let him look," he said.

Sal flung open the wagon door. An evil smell struck Highgrade in the face, a greasy blast of stench. Inside, chained to the walls while seated atop stacked cakes of lye soap and crates of bottled bleach, were three pinheads. Their skin was sallow, their dull eyes squinted against even the thin light of this gloomy dawn. They wore soiled cotton shifts and laced-up boots. Their sex was indeterminate from their facial features, but the bodies showed female characteristics. Leather bands were cinched around their middles. Through the rings in the bands were run chains that were bolted to posts in the walls.

The pinheads clapped hands, stomped feet.

"Like them?" Sal said.

Her whole body shook when she laughed and she was laughing now. Soapy gave Highgrade a horse laugh. Highgrade tore free of Sal's clutches and dashed back toward the wagon. Their laughter pursued him.

"Anybody you know?" Sal said. "Your momma, maybe?"

More scornful laughter rang out from the couple.

Slocum was back at the whiskey wagon and waiting when Highgrade returned.

"Always playing," Slocum said. "I told you to stay put and watch the wagon."

"You won't believe what I just saw!"

"What?"

"I just found out how Spellman can afford to do wash so cheap."

Slocum frowned. "What's that, more drunk talk?"

"I—no, you wouldn't believe it," Highgrade said.

"Quit canoodling and climb up here. This is a work day."

Highgrade mounted up into the wagon seat. Slocum handled the reins, hawing the mules into motion. Most of the convoy's company stood between their horses and wagons and the whiskey cart, silently watching it go. Most of the men were armed with handguns and a few shotguns. They weren't pointed at anything yet. The watchers stood silent, stone-faced.

Highgrade sniffed. "Mighty unsociable bunch."

"You just noticed, huh?"

"Nobody's leaving."

"Nobody but us," Slocum said.

"How come?"

"They made it clear through their spokesman, Orkus, that they don't want us around."

"Why not?"

"Probably heard about your shenanigans," Slocum said.

Softness brushed his eyelashes, tickled his cheek. He looked up. Fat white flakes fell from the clouds.

"It's snowing," Highgrade said.

12

The gulch rose in a series of broad flat terraces. The trail switchbacked across the slopes. When the wagon reached the first flat level, Slocum looked back. Activity swarmed in the camp of the convoy.

"Looks like they're getting ready to move out," Highgrade said.

Wet snow clung to cold ground, powdering. How strong could an April storm be? Strong enough—this was the mountains. As yet, however, the snowfall had only begun.

It was an inch deep by the time the wagon crested the top of the gulch. A panoramic view opened to the south. The bases of still higher peaks hemmed in the plateau on the east and west, flanking a broad open trough leading to the north. Vivid gray clouds bellied low, shrouding the pinnacle tops. Snowflakes swirled, billowed, tumbled.

An antlike column crawled up the lower slopes of the gulch. The convoy.

"They're moving now," Highgrade said.

"Sure. They don't want to be snowed in. They just don't want to be too close to us," Slocum said. "Smart. Orkus is using us as a stalking horse. If outlaws lie in wait, they'll jump us first. The convoy'll hear the shooting and be forewarned. If we get through, we'll have opened the way for them. If not, at least we'll have softened up the ambushers for the convoy to finish off. And if we get plugged, our whiskey is up for grabs."

Highgrade laughed so hard that he nearly fell off his seat.

"What's so damned funny?" Slocum said.

"Talk about the biter bit—! Orkus is giving you a taste of your own medicine," Highgrade said. "You used me as bait to decoy those killers back at the camp, now he's using you to flush out the killers on the road! How d'you like it when the shoe's on the other foot?"

"It must have slipped your mind that whatever happens to me is going to happen to you."

Highgrade stopped laughing. "That's a sobering thought, Slocum."

"The beauty part of it from Orkus's viewpoint is that all he's got to do is hang back and follow. We can't afford to lose time by standing still. First load of redeye to the mining camp is the one that fetches top dollar, and I mean to be first!"

The wagon advanced, threading the shallow trough that wound north through the high mountains. Inside the gorge, winds fell to whispers, and the snow fell straight down rather than in the slanted sheets prevailing in more open ground. The mules forged ahead, steady-paced, surefooted.

Firetree Gulch was lost behind a bend of the trail. On went the wagon. A gap opened in the west cliff face. Gusts howled through it with such force that the wagon was in danger of overturning, but Slocum fought through to the shelter of the next rock wall, where the wind was lessened.

Highgrade said, "Give me a gun."

"Why? You going to shoot Jack Frost?"

"It's no joke, Slocum. We're getting near Two Tors Col."

"That's the main pass, right?"

"Right. If anyone's fixing to jump us, that's the place they'll do it," Highgrade said.

The whiskey was wearing off him. Slocum gave him the reins, saying, "You drive."

"The gun?"

"Hold your horses."

Slocum reached into an inside breast pocket of his coat and took out a foot-long cigar, long and thick. Trailwise, he carried a waterproof box of matches. The lucifer burned bright, flame rising upright in the sheltered stillness of the rockbound passage. Slocum burned the end of the cigar, puffing it alight.

Taking out another cigar, he offered it to Highgrade. "Here."

Highgrade took it. "This ain't one of them exploding see-gars, is it?"

"If you don't want it, give it back."

"I want it. I was just wondering what prompted this sudden fit of generosity."

"What the hell, even a condemned man facing a firing squad gets a last smoke," Slocum said.

"That's a cheery thought."

Highgrade lit his cigar on the end of Slocum's. "Not a bad smoke," he said.

Movement well to the rear of the wagon caught his eye. "Thought I saw something back there," he said.

"You did," Slocum said. "A couple of riders from the convoy. They've been trailing us for miles. Keeping an eye on us, I guess, to make sure we're still alive and kicking."

Rifts in the falling snow bared the vague outlines of two mounted figures. An instant later they vanished behind a billowing white veil.

"Never mind them," Slocum said. "When trouble comes, it's going to come from in front, not behind. We can worry about those idiots later."

The trail rose and fell over a series of long shallow ridges. Snow in the hollows was not yet deep enough to slow the progress of the mules. When the wagon topped one rise, the convoy's scouts crested the following rise.

"And I bet that the convoy is on the rise behind them," Slocum said.

"They're bird-dogging us!"

"Worse than that, Highgrade. They're letting us do the bird-dogging."

Two Tors Col neared, a saddle flanked by a pair of jagged peaks. It was the summit of the stairway of long ridges. Nothing could be seen of its far side, nothing except snow falling through the emptiness framed by the cliffs.

Slocum eyed his cigar, which was half-smoked. He estimated that there was enough to last him to the end of the pass.

The wagon began climbing the final slope.

Highgrade said, "I'd feel a whole lot safer with a shooting iron in my hand."

"I wouldn't," Slocum said.

"Think I can't handle a gun? Give me one and I'll show you what I can do!"

"That's what I'm afraid of," Slocum said.

When the wagon was closer to the top of the ridge than the bottom, Slocum looked back, spying the scouts on the ridge across the Divide.

"Still with us," he said.

Searching for the convoy, he spotted a jagged black streak topping the rise two ridges behind—the vanguard of the wagon train.

Paired mountain peaks, the Two Tors, bulked large in the landscape, lofty, colossal. Near the top of the pass the soil was thinner, stony. Dwarfed pines huddled at the base of the cliffs. Above lay nothing but thousands of feet of bare rock wall, ledges and chimneys now garnished with snow. Winds blew fierce through the pass. The emptiness on the other side of the saddle might have been the end of the world.

The wagon rolled over the summit, starting down the other side. The gorge opened into a vast "park," a high mountain valley. It was oval-shaped, with the long ends running roughly north-south, bordered by ranged mountains. It resembled a bowl of snow, like one of those glass paperweights enclosing a winter scene, complete with a blizzard of swirling flakes.

Nearer, the out-curving walls of the gorge were broken and rent with titanic structural faults. House-sized boulders peppered the talus skirting the cliffs. Clefts big enough to hide whole towns gaped in the rock faces.

From one of those clefts poured a band of mounted men, rushing the wagon. On both sides of the trail, armed men popped up from the rocks, guns trained on the wagoneers. About twelve in all, split equally between horseback riders and those afoot.

"I'll do the talking," Slocum said.

"Fine," Highgrade said. "I'm struck speechless anyhow."

"I wish."

The ambushers were a rowdy, seething crew. The nearness of whiskey made their blood run hot. And captives to torment—that promised pleasant sport!

The riders fanned out on either side of the wagon. A burly black-bearded man swung in beside Slocum. One hand held the reins, the other leveled a gun on him.

"What have we got here? A wagonful of redeye! Damned thoughtful of you to bring it to us thirsty boys on a cold winter's day," he said. "I'm almost sorry I got to kill you, friend."

"You'll be a whole lot sorrier if you don't get your men out of sight," Slocum said.

He couldn't have sounded more bored.

A rider said to the black-bearded man, "What's he talking about, Rumpus?"

"Who cares?" Rumpus said. "Get down off that wagon, amigo. I don't want you bleeding on my whiskey."

"Sherm told me you were a pack of horse's asses, but he didn't tell the half of it," Slocum said.

"Sherm?" echoed Rumpus's sideman. "What do you know about Sherm?"

"Shut up, Jeeter. I'll do the talking here," Rumpus said. "Sherm's missing, stranger. Been gone all night, him and some of the others. What do you know about it? Talk fast!"

"Sherm's right behind me, along with Zack and the rest. They're with the convoy, so we've got some of our men on the inside when the trap shuts. But if the pilgrims catch sight of you men, you'll ruin the whole plan," Slocum said.

Others, not in on the play, impatient to get on with it, called to Rumpus to stop stalling and do something.

"I'll pin your ears back if you don't pipe down, you sons of bitches!" Rumpus shouted.

They quieted down. Rumpus thumbed back the hammer on the gun he held pointed at Slocum.

"I don't know what you're talking about. I don't know you, but I don't like you anyway," he said.

"You the headman here?"

"Don't you know?"

"I don't know and I don't care," Slocum said. "I'm going to show you something. If you know what it is, you'll know what to do. If you don't, you damn well better get someone who does know what it is."

"No," Rumpus said. "I don't like you."

Slocum turned back the right front flap of his long coat. "It's in this pocket," he said.

"It's not a gun," he added.

"Better not be. If it is, you'll be dead before it clears," Rumpus said.

Slocum dipped two forefingers into the inside pocket, hooking them around a thong, to which a heavier object was attached.

"Slow," Rumpus said.

The other end of the looped thong was tied to one of the wolf's paws that Slocum had found.

He said, "You savvy this, Rumpus?"

"What's that, Rumpus? Some heathen charm or something?"

"Shut up, Jeeter. Forget you saw that. That goes for the rest of you, too." He turned to Slocum. "Put it away. You made your point."

"No, I didn't," Slocum said. "Otherwise these men would be out of sight before the convoy sees 'em."

"Convoy? Bullshit! What convoy?"

"You've got spotters, don't you? Ask them if it's coming. Only make sure they don't get spotted."

Lookouts were posted on high ledges overlooking the south approach, but the sentries all had their backs turned to it as they waited for the impasse with the wagon to be resolved.

Rumpus got mad when he looked up and saw the sentries watching him. "Look the other way, you dumb bastards, and tell me what you see! And don't skyline!"

The sentries ducked, covering behind rocks as they scanned the landscape. Rumpus lowered the hammer, but kept Slocum covered. The wolf paw had long since disappeared into his pocket.

A snicker came from the rider flanking Rumpus on the side opposite Jeeter. "Can't skyline in a snowstorm," he said.

Without warning, Rumpus's arm snaked out, laying the long barrel of his gun across the other's jawline, knocking him out of the saddle.

"Keep your comment to yourself, Dix."

"He can't hear you, Rumpus, he's out cold."

"Shut up, Jeeter. Go get Hutty."

"Okay," Jeeter said. Turning his horse, he rode back into the cleft from which they had emerged.

Dix groaned, slumped on the ground. A horse stepped on him. Shouting, he rolled away, rising on his hands and knees. His jaw was swollen, marked. His face creased with pain.

"You hit me when I wasn't looking!" he said.

Rumpus pointed the gun at him. "You're looking now."

Dix threw up his arms. "No—no, don't! Don't shoot!"

At that moment one of the lookouts posted on the heights cupped a hand to his mouth, shouting, "Riders on the trail!"

"Don't shoot, they'll hear you and be warned off," Slocum said.

Rumpus holstered his gun. "This is your lucky day, Dix."

Dix staggered to his feet, clumps of show falling from him. He lurched to his horse, which another rider held by the reins. He clung to the saddle, too weak to mount up.

Jeeter returned with another rider. The newcomer was tall, thin, pale-eyed, taut. Hutty, the boss of the bunch. A coyote to Rumpus's bull. His face was long, canine.

He said, "What happened to Dix?"

"He sassed me," Rumpus said.

"Did not!" said Dix.

"You're doing it again."

"Save it for later," Hutty said. To Slocum he said, "Talk."

"Not so fast," Slocum said. "I've shown my calling card, now let's see yours."

Apparently Jeeter had brought Hutty up-to-date, for he asked no questions. He pulled a wolf's paw from his clothes.

"Satisfied?" Hutty said.

Slocum nodded.

Hutty put away the talisman. "Now, talk," he said.

"I'm Slocum. This is my partner, Highgrade."

"Never heard of you."

"I never heard of you, either, Hutty, so that makes us even. That's what the paws are for, ain't it?"

Hutty shrugged. "Somebody said something about a convoy."

"It's right behind me," Slocum said. "Ellis set it up. Talked a bunch of pilgrims into making the trek together. That's what took so long, rounding them all up in one group. They thought Deacon was doing them a favor. Even gave them a group discount on the toll."

"Funny, huh?" Highgrade said.

Hutty ignored him. "You're Deacon's man?"

"Not hardly. I'm my own man," Slocum said.

"Why'd Deacon send you?"

"He didn't. I was heading this way myself, so I volunteered to pass the word. He's kind of shorthanded now. Had a dust-up with some citizens who thought they could cross for free. Lost some men."

"Where's my men?"

"Sherm and the rest are riding along with the convoy. Deacon sold them that they'd be good medicine against outlaws. When the shooting starts, they'll be right in the middle of the enemy camp," Slocum said.

He glanced back, looking the way he came.

"That convoy'll be coming along any minute now," he said.

"There's scouts out, too."

"The spotters seen them scouts, Hutty," said Rumpus.

"We've got time," Hutty said. "They can't see us on this side of the saddle until they're right on top of it."

"If the scouts warn them first—" Slocum said.

"The sentries will sing out before they get too close," Hutty said.

The lookouts reported that the scouts had reached the midpoint of the divide.

"Something's topping the far rise," a sentry shouted. "It's a wagon—no—a line of wagons!"

"I see it, too!" another said.

"Hot damn!" Jeeter said, rubbing his hands.

"Told you so," Highgrade said.

Hutty swung into action. "You riders, get back out of sight and stay there till you get the signal! Riflemen, get behind those rocks on both sides of the trail! You others, you know what to do, so get to it! *Move!*"

They moved. Hutty said, "Snake that wagon into the pocket where it'll be out of sight!"

"Like hell," Slocum said.

Hutty assumed his best don't-try-me expression. "I don't have time to fool with you—"

"Then don't. You've got your job, I've got mine. Mine is to get this wagon through, not get mixed up with an ambush."

"You'll be safe here."

"I'll be safer over the hill, which is where I'm going. Time's a-wasting. If I don't deliver on time, it's my scalp."

"Who gets the redeye?"

"If you don't know, I'm not going to tell you," Slocum said. "Here's another thing: If the scouts see the wagon ahead on the trail, they'll figure it's clear sailing all the way through. But if they don't see it, they'll know something's wrong."

"He's got something there," Rumpus said.

"All right," said Hutty, "you can go."

"I'm gone," Slocum said, gathering up the reins.

Rumpus said, "How 'bout leaving one of them barrels here to keep us warm?"

"Why don't you just take the lifeblood from my veins? That's what'll happen to me anyhow if the load comes up short," Slocum said.

Rumpus laughed. "I know what you mean."

"It'll be plenty warm around here when that convoy shows up," Slocum said.

"For them."

Hutty said, "What kind of firepower are those pilgrims packing?"

"Nothing to speak of. Just a pack of old men and boys with a few rusty handguns," Slocum lied.

"It'll be a turkey shoot!" Rumpus said.

"Yah." Slocum started the team, and the wagon began the descent. Highgrade flipped a half wave, half salute at the outlaw chiefs. Rumpus nodded. Leaning over in the saddle, Hutty hurriedly conferred with the black-bearded man.

"I don't like the looks of that," Highgrade said.

"Quit gawking and face front, you'll look less guilty that way," Slocum said.

"Let me take the reins, free up your hands."

"Not yet."

Highgrade sat hunched up, leaning far forward to provide less of a target to riflemen back at the pass. He held himself tight in expectation of a bullet crashing into him at any second.

The slope leveled, spilling the trail on to the floor of the park. The snowfall was beginning to drift up, but there wasn't enough of it yet to impede the progress of the mules. It rolled across the valley in wavelets like scalloped surf breaking on a beach. Steam spewed from the mules' snouts.

Hoofbeats pounded behind them, nearing. Two riders from the outlaw camp.

"Give me a gun," Highgrade pleaded.

"Simmer down. They're not shooting. Their guns aren't even drawn," Slocum said.

The riders slowed, pulling abreast of the wagon, which continued on its way. One of the duo was Jeeter. The other was a heavyset older man with a scar over the corner of his mouth that made him look as if he were sneering.

"Hutty got worried about you boys, so he sent Vince and me to see you safely out of the park," Jeeter said.

"Mighty thoughtful of him," said Slocum. "No worry about being shorthanded for the ambush?"

"If they run into trouble, we'll hear it and rush back," Jeeter said.

"How about a taste?" Vince said.

"No can do," Slocum said.

"Shit, you got a wagonful, you can spare a leetle."

"See me when I get where I'm going and I'll give you a free shot," Slocum said.

"I'm thirsty now."

"You and me both, brother," Highgrade said. "This hombre's so tight with the whiskey you'd think it was his!"

"What would Hutty do if you dragged down some of the loot from a holdup without sharing it with the rest of the gang?" Slocum said.

"Why, he'd skin us alive," Jeeter said.

"I'm in the same boat with the whiskey."

"I take your point. Who's your contact at the mining camp?"

"Didn't Hutty tell you?"

"Well, now, it must have slipped his mind."

"If he didn't tell you, you won't get it from me," Slocum said.

A stream wound through the valley, cutting the trail at midpoint. A wooden plank bridge spanned it. Trees grew along the banks on both sides, their bare trunks and branches knitted into black lacework trimming the snowy landscape. The ice-edged stream ran clear and dark in its center.

"Reckon that convoy'll be rolling through any minute now," Jeeter said.

"You're going to miss the fun," Slocum said.

Jeeter shrugged. "You never can tell." He and Vince exchanged glances. "Hutty said for us to see you out of the park and that's what we'll do," Jeeter said.

The head of the mule train neared the bridge. Woods on both sides of the trail partially screened the scene from open view. Slocum reined in the team to a halt.

Jeeter said, "Why you stopping here?"

"Because I don't want the bridge to collapse under me," Slocum said. "Go check those planks, Highgrade. Make sure they're not rotten."

Highgrade climbed down, hesitant, unsure. A pair of stout beams spanned the stream banks. Planks were nailed down across them. They were snow-covered except for the spaces between the planks, which were black slits. There were no safety rails. Highgrade made a show of peering down at the supports, stamping around on the bridge.

"Looks all right to me," he said.

"Good," Slocum said. "Now, to get these balky mules moving again."

Gripping the bullwhip by the haft, he let it uncoil, spilling the blacksnake on the ground. He shook out his wrist to loosen it, then trailed out his arm back behind him, drawing the long whip clear so that he would have plenty of room to wield it. Swinging his arm, he slung the blacksnake not in the air above the mules' heads, but to the side, so it wrapped around

Jeeter's neck. A twist of the wrist pulled it tight, so the black windings cut deep into the man's throat. Jeeter's eyes bulged. He grabbed for the taut whip with both hands. Slocum yanked him off his horse.

Vince reached for his gun. Slocum dove off the side of the wagon at him. A satisfying *oof!* sounded when his shoulder slammed into Vince's middle, knocking him sideways off his horse. Vince hit the ground hard. Slocum landed on top of him. The horse upreared, whinnying, pawing the ground.

Slocum pulled his boot knife and buried it in Vince's heart. Light died out of Vince's staring eyes; his bellowed outrage became his death rattle.

Slocum rose on one knee, turning toward Jeeter. Jeeter was on his feet, crouching, still trailing the whip from where it was wrapped around his neck. A gun was in his hand, but the riderless horses blocked a clear shot at Slocum. Tearing with his free hand at the rawhide coiled around his neck, he hunched low, head bobbing, trying to see through the horses' legs.

Slocum threw himself flat, rolling sideways, clear of the horses. Standing on one knee, he pointed his left arm out at Jeeter, who was turning toward him. Right hand wrapping the cold blade, Slocum bent back his arm until the knife was over his shoulder, then threw it.

The blade struck home, lodging deep in the center of Jeeter's chest. He recoiled, rising on tiptoe, staring down in horror at the knife sticking out from his torso like a handle. He jerked the trigger; a shot boomed. He was already falling when he fired it, so it went nowhere. Echoes from the report spread outward across the park, like ripples from a pebble dropped into a pond.

Slocum retrieved the knife, wiping it clean on Jeeter's shoulder before returning it to its boot-top sheath. Highgrade stood to one side at the head of the mule team, holding the harnesses to keep the animals from bolting. In truth, the mules were not particularly upset; life on the Blue Meadow-Bishop's Ford-Kettle run was inuring them to gunfire, bloodshed, and sudden death. Highgrade was shaky, though.

Slocum climbed up on the box, stuffing the whip to one side, taking up the reins. Highgrade joined him, huffing and puffing.

Slocum said, "The fat's in the fire now!"

Throwing the handbrake that he had surreptitiously set after stopping the wagon, Slocum hawed the team toward the bridge. Hoofbeats and rolling wheels rumbled against the planks as the span shuddered under the weight of team and wagon. From bridge to water was only a four-foot drop, and the stream was no more than two or three feet deep at its center, but if the bridge collapsed the run was over. It would take hours to extricate the wagon from the streambed, time that Hutty's gang was unlikely to grant.

A board broke under the left front wheel. The wagon rolled on. Left and right wheels dipped into the space made by the splintered plank, catching for a heart-stopping instant, then tearing free as the vehicle's forward momentum pulled it past the gap. The team was on solid ground on the other side of the bridge and they drew the wagon along with them.

Gunfire crackled far behind them, *pop pop pop*. Then more pops. A bend in the trail threw a screen of woods between the wagon and Two Tors Col. The wagon barreled through the curves, nearly ejecting Highgrade at a sharp turn. Slocum caught him by the back of the neck and kept him from falling out. Highgrade hung on tight.

The woods ended, replaced by a gentle slope rising to the narrow north end of the park. When the wagon had risen above the trees, Slocum looked back.

Gunfire continued popping back at the pass. Puffs of gunsmoke hung in the air, blurred figures crawling over jumbled rocks.

"Not shooting at us," Slocum said. "The convoy must have reached the pass, or the scouts, anyhow. Jeeter's shot set off the whole shebang, ready or not."

"They coming after us?"

Slocum glanced back, not stopping the wagon for a better look. "They've got their hands full with the convoy. When they find out just what kind of a tiger they've got by the tail, it'll be too late. Riflemen'll pick 'em off from the heights if they run."

"That war' a close one!"

"Jeeter and Vince would've thrown down on us as soon as we were safely away from the pass," Slocum said.

"Reckon they knew we wasn't really in the outfit?"

"No. They'd have hit us at the pass. Hutty was thirsty, that's all. He didn't mind crossing the outfit on the QT. Jeeter and Vince would get rid of us with no witnesses. They might have had a private deal with Hutty to keep it a secret and cheat their own gang out of it."

Fresh volleys erupted in the pass, louder, stronger.

"There's Orkus's guns now," Slocum said. "Sounds like a battle royale. We're well out of it."

When the wagon reached the far end of the valley, snow had covered its tracks from the bridge to the pass. Gunfire continued, muted by distance, but undiminished in ferocity.

Highgrade rubbed his face, his hands coming away wet. He mopped himself with a filthy bandanna. "Can you beat that? I'm sweating . . . sweating in the middle of a snowstorm!"

"Sweating booze," Slocum said.

"Maybe—maybe! The way you bluffed them outlaws, I'm lucky I ain't pissed in my pants! What would you have done if Hutty hadn't fallen for that trick with the wolf's paw?"

"I'd have used my fallback plan."

Slocum pulled back a flap of his coat, baring an inside pocket bulging with a bundle of dynamite, its fuses entwined.

Highgrade took it badly. "You loco—! We could've got blowed sky-high with all your jumping and wrassling and whatnot!"

"They're tame. No blasting caps."

"Then what good are they?"

"Plenty, when it comes to scaring folks who don't know that they're not primed," Slocum said.

"Yeah, well, it's a good thing that bluff of yours took, that's all I got to say."

"It's not enough to shoot, Highgrade, you've got to be able to think on your feet."

"And if that don't work?"

"Shoot!"

The park ended in a wide, flat-floored ravine that angled right, then left. Once the second curve was rounded, the gunshots became inaudible.

"Whew," Highgrade said, slumping with relief. "I thought we'd never get shut of that place!"

Slocum laughed. "Could have been worse. Suppose Fitch or his pal were there to tell the gang what really happened down to the ford?"

Highgrade paled under his wind-burned ruddiness. "I forgot about them!"

"I didn't. If they'd've been at the pass, it'd've been Katie bar the door!"

They rolled on. The ravine widened into a second mountain valley. "The Kettle's the next one after this," Highgrade said.

"In that case, I'll put the blasting caps back in!"

13

It was snowing in Singwell, Colorado, at midday when the San Francisco express reached the end of the line.

A map of the railroads in this part of the mountains would have resembled a sketch of a tree pruned by a drunken gardener. From the trunk line on the flat, branches fanned out through the range, throwing out offshoots that abruptly terminated at this isolated plateau or that lofty cirque valley cul-de-sac. There was an underlying logic behind the seemingly haphazard distribution of the lines, a calculus of dollars and cents. The railroads would build a line to anywhere where money could be made. In this locale, that meant mining, whether of precious metals such as gold and silver, or of less spectacular ores, such as copper or lead.

Singwell was the closest rail approach to the Kettle. The tracks terminated on an 8,500-foot-high stony ledge northwest of the park. Connecting the sites was Hollander's Chute, a twisty worm run between the peaks. Back in the days of the California gold rush, a party of forty-niners had been snowed in at the Kettle for the winter. Came the thaw, and the forlorn handful of survivors were finally able to escape their stone prison by the chute. When they broke out onto the western ledge, they were greeted by birds warbling in the trees. "The birds sing well here," said one of the party, and so the place gained its name, Singwell.

A handful of buildings squatted in the lee of a rocky limb near the railroad yard—that was the town proper. "Town" was almost too grandiose a word for the threadbare settlement. But the gold rush had set it swarming with frenzied gold seekers.

The site was crowded even before the express disgorged its human cargo.

Blackie Hawkins stood on the rear platform of the private car, taking in the scene as he pulled on a pair of thin black leather gloves. He wore a stiff-brim hat and a long coat. Fat wet flakes swirled about him; gusty winds tugged at his coat flaps, playing peek-a-boo with the twin guns belted on his hips. Pale from a life lived largely away from daylight, his face had color stung into it by the cold.

Most of his men were seeing to the unloading of horses and supplies from the boxcar coupled in tandem with the private car; a few higher-ups hovered nearby in his orbit. Boxcar doors were flung open. A crash sounded as the loading ramp hit the ground. A moment later horses were being led down the ramp to the platform.

Hawkins looked around for his local contacts, not finding them. That meant nothing. They were cautious men, as men must be when the law has put a price on their heads.

The railroad platform seethed with activity. Passengers raced up and down, portmanteaus in hand, seeking some sort of transportation to the gold fields. An even larger group of entrepreneurs was on hand to greet them, hawking everything from horses to supplies to mining claims. The eddying mass of bodies formed up into knots of would-be buyers and sellers. Meanwhile, freight cars were emptied of horses and supplies, multiplying the tumult.

Glancing casually back into the private car, Hawkins did a take, struck by the absence of that which he expected to see. He went inside, where a man was prying open the lid of a crate of ammunition.

Hawkins said, "Where's Schlemmer?"

The other shrugged. "He was just here a minute ago."

"I know where he is," Hawkins said.

He went down the aisle to the far end of the car. It was quicker than bulling his way through the crowded platform, but somehow he knew that it was still too late.

Outside, Moira Connell waited while Dmitri handled the unloading of the six horses she had brought from San Francisco. She wore a round fur hat, a gray-green coat with fur collar and cuffs, gloves, a long skirt, boots. Belinda Gale stood nearby. Off to one side was Julian Roux, wrapped in the folds of a coat that was too big for him. He suspected it was Dmitri's. It was warm, though. The collar was turned up, the buttons were fastened, and Julian's hands were hidden inside the pockets. Cold, snow, and stony peaks formed a combination that he found fresh and bracing.

Schlemmer found him. He was on the other side of the train. He emerged from between two cars farther up along the consist. If he hoped to surprise Roux, he was disappointed, for the gambler had turned to face him when he stepped into view on the platform. Schlemmer, undaunted, kept on coming forward, not hurrying, but deliberate. He stopped about ten feet away from Roux. He'd come outside without a heavy coat, clad in a dark suit and white shirt more appropriate for the Savoy Club. He rubbed his hands and blew on them, keeping them warm. His holstered gun was tied down to his leg, ready for action.

Hawkins reached the scene as the two men faced off. It was too late for him to do anything but watch and wait as the confrontation played itself out.

Schlemmer said, "Have a nice trip?"

"I've been expecting you," Julian said.

Schlemmer nodded. Snowflakes clung to the tips of his white waxed mustache for an instant before melting.

He said, "What'll you do now, without Blackie to protect you?"

"Kill you, Schlemmer."

Schlemmer reached for his gun. Julian's hand lifted under the coat, thrusting a gun barrel into view. He fired into Schlemmer's middle. Schlemmer jackknifed, face contorted, mouth open but unable to cry out as he spilled to the platform.

It was all over before anybody nearby had even known that a showdown was in progress. After the echoes of the shot died away, men ducked for cover and a woman screamed—not Moira or Belinda Gale.

Julian's free hand unbuttoned his coat, opening it. The pockets had been cut out, giving his hands freedom of movement. He had had the gun in his hand all the while, held hidden under his coat along his side. At the moment of truth, he'd merely raised the gun and fired before Schlemmer's gun had cleared the holster.

Schlemmer lay in a heap, not even twitching, stone dead. Julian stepped back a few paces, gun leveled, ready for all comers. Hawkins stepped into the breach before any of his men could accept the challenge.

"Back off," he said, and they did.

"I asked you not to kill him, Julian."

"You didn't keep him away from me, Blackie."

Hawkins nodded. "When a damned fool is set on getting himself killed, there's no stopping him."

He noticed that some of his hirelings were still in place, watching.

"What are you lollygaggling at? Get back to your duties," he said. They dispersed to their various tasks.

Moira's face was tight about the mouth and eyes; Belinda Gale stared into the distance. The lead rope of the string of horses was gripped by one of Dmitri's hands; in the other was the sawed-off shotgun. Hawkins smiled without parting his lips.

"Put it away, Dmitri," Moira said. "We're in no danger from this, ah, gentleman."

When the double-barreled blaster was safely pointing downward, Hawkins tipped his hat to the ladies.

"Good day, Miss Moira."

"Fancy meeting you here, Blackie."

"You're a long ways from home."

"You, too. Come to enjoy the healthy mountain air?"

Hawkins laughed. "It's about to get decidedly unhealthy for some people."

"You'll see to that, I'm sure," she said.

"Be sure. There's a bunch of hardheaded squatters in the gold fields who don't have the sense to clear out while they still can."

"But you'll make them see the light, eh?"

"That's what I'm hired to do," he said.

"Hired? By who?"

"Big men. You probably know some of them yourself,"

Hawkins said. "I'd hate to see you get caught in the crossfire, Miss Moira."

"That a threat?" Julian said.

"Just a word to the wise," said Hawkins.

"I'm not worried," Moira said, "not with Julian as my bodyguard."

"We'll see," Hawkins said. "Nice running into you, Miss Moira. We'll meet again, I'm sure."

He turned to Roux. "That the gun I gave you, Julian?"

"Yes. Want it back?"

"Keep it. You'll need it," Hawkins said.

He walked away, back toward the rear of the train. Moira looked from him, to Schlemmer, to Julian.

She said, "What was that all about, Julian?"

"Schlemmer's been itching for a showdown for a long time now, and he finally got one."

"I'll say," Belinda Gale said.

If there was any lawman in Singwell, he was unconcerned with the killing, since no inquiries were made. Now that the shooting had stopped, with no sign of an immediate renewal, things returned to normal. A number of onlookers gawked at the corpse, but the vast majority thronging the railroad yard went about their business.

Three riders had sat their horses atop a nearby rise, watching the shooting and its aftermath. As the scene resumed its former hustle and bustle, they rode down to the train, to the private car. The man in the middle dismounted, handing the reins to a sideman.

A big man, he wore a campaign hat and a blue-gray cloth coat with a wolfskin collar. The hat had a peaked crown and a flat brim. His face was almost as wide as it was long. Brown-eyed, leathery, stubbled with a three-day beard. Crescent nose and a wide lipless mouth. The mouth turned down at one corner and quirked up at the other, giving him a sardonic look.

Two San Francisco gunmen stood between him and the private car. When he told his name, they stepped aside to let him pass. He went up the stairs and inside.

Heads turned as the occupants eyed him. "I'm Proctor," he announced.

Blackie Hawkins went to him, the others went back to what they were doing.

"I'm Hawkins."

Proctor nodded. The duo appraised each other, searching for weaknesses, finding none.

"How goes it?" Hawkins said.

"All set on this end. We've been waiting on you."

"Here I am."

"When do we go?"

"As soon as my men are mounted up."

"Good," Proctor said. "What about that shooting just now?"

"That's got nothing to do with this."

"One of your men got killed," Proctor said.

"Saved me the trouble of killing him myself, for disobeying orders. I told him not to go picking fights."

"And the other? Who was he? He was fast."

"He belongs to me. He's on a long leash, that's all," Hawkins said.

During the last Ice Age, a glacier carved out the steep-sided, bowl-shaped valley known as the Kettle. It was about fifty square miles in area. At the north of the cirque were three peaks set back from each other on a diagonal line, Mts. Shadrach, Meshack, and Abend-nego. A stream rising from its source high on Mt. Shadrach fell hundreds of feet to the park floor below. This was Long Falls, named after Major Stephen H. Long, the explorer whose name also graces Long's Peak. He didn't discover the falls. One of his scouts did. Such is fame. Notch Pass was the eastern gateway to the Kettle, joined to the flat by Bearclaw Trail. The southwest wall of the valley was broken by a gorge that was the last stretch of the corridor winding through the range to Firetree Gulch and then downward to the crossing at Big Elk Creek. In the northwest was Hollander's Chute, passage to the Singwell railhead at the Divide.

The valley was heavily wooded with shaggy evergreens. A creek ran from Long Falls southeast across the park, fed by smaller streams, laying down a fan-shaped tracery of waterways. Now, mining camps and prospectors' tents dotted the land throughout the watercourse, much of which had the rawness of recently cleared sites, worm runs coiling through the big trees. There were some cabins but mostly tents. Most of the timber had been felled for the gold seekers' sluices and to shore up excavations. Patches of stubbly tree stumps mottled the bowl of blue-green forest like mange.

Moira Connell's party on horseback broke out of Hollander's Chute into the Kettle at late afternoon. It was still snowing; six to eight inches of the white stuff had already fallen. It magnified what was left of the daylight. Riders and supply horses were strung out in a line pointed at Mt. Shadrach. Moira and Belinda Gale rode not sidesaddle, but straddling their mounts. Julian Roux rode point. Dmitri brought up the rear.

Long Falls was a silver strand stretched upright against black rock walls, beckoning the travelers through a flurry of windborne flakes. At its foot was a large natural basin, three hundred feet long, seventy-five feet wide, with up-curving banks about ten feet high. It was filled with black water fed by the falls. Water spilled from a V-shaped notch in the embankment, the source for the creek that meandered across the valley floor.

The riders halted on a ledge jutting from the rock face west of the basin, level with the lip. The banks were ten feet tall, but there was no telling how deep or shallow was the basin floor, since the water was inky black, opaque, impenetrable. An icy column marked the cliff with the path of the falls. Water dribbled down it into the basin, kicking up spumes of spray where it hit the water.

Moira said, "We're here."

"Where's your holdings?" Julian said.

"There." Moira pointed at the basin.

Throwing back his head, Julian laughed loud and long. "I don't mean to be rude, but you must see the humor in it."

"Not really," Moira said coolly.

"Here we are, at the site of the richest gold strike in Colorado since the war, and your piece of it is under water! I'm sorry, but you've made this trip for nothing, Moira."

"That shows what you know, or rather what you don't know, gambler. Mining requires water, to pan out color from the streams, not to mention large-scale operations. The late Mr. Connell knew that, that's why he bought up this property. A small dam with a watergate at that spillway will let me control the water supply for the whole Kettle. Every prospector camped out on the creek will have to pay me for water rights. If they don't I'll shut off the flow of water and dry up the creek, putting them all out of business. I've got the whole valley and everybody in it by the balls," she said.

Julian whistled. "That's some scheme! But what makes you think the miners will sit still for it?"

"That's what I've got you for."

"Very flattering, but I'm just one man against many."

"You'll organize a gang of gunmen. There won't be any shortage of hard cases looking to turn a fast dollar. I'll hire them and you'll ramrod them. We won't tip our hand until we've got the firepower to back our play."

"It could work . . . if you live long enough."

"Your job is to see that I do," Moira said. "And that's not all. Once we've milked the water rights for every last cent, the basin can be drained and mined for gold. Or sold."

"You'll set the Kettle boiling, Moira."

"Let it. I don't give a damn who gets burned, as long as I get mine."

"And the other fellow's, too, eh?"

"That's right," she said. "Too bad Blackie's such a snake. His outfit would be perfect for what I've got in mind."

"Forget it, Moira. He's got other fish to fry," Julian said.

The Kettle bubbled with noise and motion.

Calling out to a stranger racing past, a man asked, "What's all the excitement, bub?"

"It's the Redeye Express!"

"Wha'—?! Wait for me!"

But there was no waiting, for in the procurement of fresh whiskey, as in other things, it was first come, first served.

Placer miners were staked out on the streams and creeks that showed color or at least hinted at the promise of same. Others, who had hit a gold vein or had hopes of doing so, had laid their claims out on parcels of land. To serve the gold seekers, and/or fleece them, a town had sprung up overnight. It was located in the center of the valley, squatting on both sides of a road that was a continuation of the Bearclaw Trail. A few structures were made of beams and boards that had been freighted up from the flat. A few more were cabins whose logs had been hewn from local trees. Most were canvas tents, about forty or more, a "ragtown" settlement.

There was a supply store or two, a "café" whose prime-cut steaks were more often than not horse meat, an assay office set up in a one-room shack by Bissell of Blue Meadow, and a few other establishments. Ragtown was devoted to relieving the miners of their hard-won gold dust and nuggets via whores, gambling, and hooch. The tent city averaged a murder a day, plus countless shootings, stabbings, and brawls that did not result in fatalities.

Now, whores and tinhorns were more plentiful than ever, creating a buyer's market, but the supply of rotgut whiskey was seriously diminished, commanding its highest prices ever. Hard drinking came as naturally to the miners as breathing, while the gamblers and whores relied on it to soften up their marks, as well as solacing their own private hurts.

It was in this climate that Slocum and Highgrade arrived with the whiskey wagon, the "Redeye Express." Dusk was falling along with snowflakes when they set up for business on a patch of ground between the wood buildings and the tent city. A crowd quickly gathered, drawn as much by a hunger for novelty as by a thirst for whiskey. More were arriving with every moment. Part auction, part carnival, and part chaos, the proceedings were about to begin.

Off to one side, where they'd been dragged out of the way, lay four men, all wounded, some dying. They were toughs who'd tried to take their whiskey without paying. The next thing they knew, Slocum's guns were in his hands, blasting them down. "That'll teach 'em to mind their manners," Slocum had said.

After that, the crowd of would-be buyers was less inclined to push itself forward. A half-dozen burly characters armed with pick and ax handles were hired by Slocum to forestall a whiskey-looting rush by the crowd. They'd be paid in whiskey when the job was done. Not much; but then, even a little was worth a lot in this climate of scarcity. Slocum wanted to pay them in cash but they refused. Whiskey was the coin of choice.

Torches on the ends of long poles hammered into the ground around the wagon lit the scene, fluttering in the wind. Slocum cautioned against placing them too close to the barrels in the hopper. "This stuff is volatile," he said. "It'd go up like a tinderbox!"

A barrel was set on the ground near the back of the wagon. Its top would serve as a table on which Highgrade would examine the dust and nuggets offered in payment for redeye. A shotgun stood near at hand, and a six-gun jutted out of the top of his pants.

He said, "Save me a jugful and sell off the rest, Slocum."

"You're getting reformed, Highgrade."

"Hell, no! With what I make here, I can stay drunk for a month down on the flat!"

"We're just about ready to start. I'm going to sell off the stuff as fast as I can—while still getting top dollar, of course. If somebody wants the whole load and can meet my price, he can have it. If not, I'll auction it off barrel by barrel. After that, we clear out fast. The way we came is the best bet, now that it's been cleared of outlaws," Slocum said.

"Reckon the convoy made it through?"

"I don't see 'em yet, but they'll be along directly, Highgrade."

"Better get the show on the road."

"Yah, and then we'll get on the road."

Rufe had already arrived. He'd been one of the scouts sent ahead of the wagon train. He had a bad feeling about the pass. Hairs rose on the back of his neck, prompted by the presence of the unseen. There was a sense of lurkers hidden behind the rocks. A whinny sounded, abruptly cut off. It came from deep within a cleft in the rocks. "Hear that?" his companion whispered. "I didn't hear nothing," he said. It was all he could do to keep from spurring his horse into a run. Many tracks of horses and men marked the snowy ground of the pass, far more than those that had exited it down the slope. Movement rustled on either side, motion flickered in the corners of his eyes. He held his head rigid, staring straight ahead. Bushwhackers lay in wait, he knew, but they held their fire for fear of alerting the convoy. Very well, he would take advantage of that fact. Waving to the wagoneers farther back on the trail, he signaled that everything was all-clear. "I don't like it," his companion said. "You like being dead better?" he retorted. "Just keep on riding and make like everything's hunky-dory and we just might get out of this alive." They reached the pass as the head of the caravan entered it. Far below, at the bottom of the slope, a wagon and some riders disappeared into the woods on the other side of the stream. A shot sounded. Rufe ducked low, spurring his horse hard. Gunfire broke out in the pass. Bullets cut the air near Rufe but not many; none by the time he reached the bottom of the hill. Afraid to cross the bridge, he hid in the woods on his side of the stream. It was then that he noticed his companion's horse was riderless. The corpse lay sprawled on the ground about a third of the way down from the pass.

A half mile east of the bridge, Rufe found a place where he could ford the stream. He rode north toward the Kettle, skirting the main road, skulking in the brush alongside it. Daylight was closing fast as he reached the tent city. Hitching his horse to a tree, he roamed the outskirts of the crowd, drawn as much by curiosity as by an urge to lose himself in the warm anonymity of the gathering.

Accidentally jostling a stranger, he muttered his apologies. "Excuse me," said the other.

Rufe recognized him. *"Fitch!"*

Fitch didn't remember the partner of the youth he'd gunned down yesterday at the ford, but he knew trouble when it called him by name. He threw himself back into the ranks of the crowd as Rufe pulled his gun and fired.

Rufe emptied his gun in Fitch's direction, missing his target, but hitting five innocent bystanders. Screams, shouts, pandemonium as the wounded and the slain tumbled into snowy ground to redden it with their blood.

Rufe didn't stick around to try to explain himself. He took

to his heels and ran, protected by the chaos that prevented him from being pursued as the crazed gunman who had blindly unloaded into the crowd. It all happened so fast that he had vanished into the maze of tents before the raising of a hue and cry.

Animal cunning returned after that first blind fight. Slowing, shaking, he forced himself to walk, not run. Running was an admission of guilt. A roundabout route would take him to his horse, and then escape.

No sooner had he emerged from ragtown than a murderous onslaught began.

Mounted men charged the settlement from all sides, dozens of them, firing into the crowd. Unlike Rufe's, their attack had purpose, direction, and sustained firepower. They rode down on the town like gun-bearing Furies.

A line of horsemen were coming straight at him. Rufe threw himself headfirst into a ditch, cowering there as hoofbeats pounded the earth near him.

The ambush at Two Tors Col had been sprung prematurely, before more than the head of the column had entered the pass. The rest of the convoy was spared the outlaws' deadly crossfire. They took cover and shot back, unleashing a vicious firefight. After an initial stalemate, the wagoneers began turning the tide, steadily felling more outlaws. A few outlaws tried to desert under fire; they were cut down by Rumpus and Hutty. But the brigand leaders were bucking majority will. Their men didn't shy from a little gunplay, but a fair fight with a well-armed, well-ordered foe was a horse of a different color. That wasn't robbery, it was work; dangerous work that could get a man killed. Hutty decided to call a retreat before the situation degenerated into a rout.

A rear guard laid down a barrage of covering fire while the others made their break. The ambushers rode out of the cleft, leaving the pass behind as they galloped down the hill. Convoy sharpshooters managed to pick off a few before they were out of range. The rear guard had already been slain, shot down as they mounted up to make their getaway.

Among those who lived to cross the bridge were Hutty and

Rumpus, strong survivor types. The tattered remnants of the gang rode hard, up the hill, through the ravine, and into the nameless park. There, they left the trail, angling to the right. At the northeastern corner of the park, hidden by trees, was a crack in the rock, an obscure passage into the Kettle, little known to honest travelers but familiar indeed to the outlaws plaguing the region. So narrow was the gap that a horse could barely pass through it without brushing its flanks against the rock walls. It opened into a pine forest in the southeast corner of the Kettle.

Nearby was the main base of all the outlaw gangs. From this hidden fort they could ride down to the Kettle floor, to the Bearclaw Trail, or to the nameless park and the pass. About a dozen men were in camp. They were outraged by the routing of their fellows. High time they showed the Kettle who was boss!

Tollin Proctor was chief of all the outlaws swearing allegiance to the Wolfpaw gang. He was absent, gone with two sidemen to meet the Californians at Singwell.

"We can do the job ourselves," Hutty said.

"We'd better," Rumpus said in an aside, "or Proctor'll have our heads for showing our backs at the pass."

Twelve at the camp plus Hutty's bunch made twenty in all, twenty killers who rode out armed to the teeth. Massing at the edge of the pines, they sent runners down to town, to tip others of the gang who were in place there.

Close to a foot of wet snow had already fallen, obstructing a wild rush down the slope into the town. By twos and threes the outlaws filtered into the outskirts of town, forming into a line when the last man was in place. Then they charged, riders of the snowstorm.

Like an iron scythe they swept through the heart of the tent city, tearing it down, trampling it. Anyone they saw, they killed. That wasn't many, since most of the inhabitants were clustered around the whiskey wagon for the start of the auction. Outnumbering the outlaws by twenty-five to one, they were nonetheless easy pickings for the ferocious surprise attack. As the first shots riddled those on its fringes, the crowd atomized into a swarm of individuals running for their lives.

It was slaughter, pure slaughter, for those caught in the first rush. Holding the reins in their teeth, the outlaws fired with both hands, emptying their guns. The mass of the dense-packed mob broke the charge, stampeding every which way as the outlaws paused to reload. Those who wanted to shoot back couldn't at first, due to the press of bodies surrounding them.

Flames leapt up as ragtown was put to the torch. Canvas burned hot and fast. Winds fed the fire, fanning it to a super-heated inferno. Human torches ran screaming from the blaze, falling with a hiss of steam into the snowbanks.

"Forget about the auction, you can pay me now," Highgrade said.

Slocum didn't answer. He was too busy levering his shoul-dered Winchester, blasting outlaws out of the saddle. Had they all charge en masse, he would have been done for, but when their first rush was broken by the bodies of the crowd, they dispersed into smaller groups, each going where the mood took them. Some chased fugitives, shooting them in the back, running them down under their horses' hooves when they ran out of bullets. Others pursued women, to rape and mur-der. Others raided the wooden buildings, looting and burning.

Out of the darkness a rider bore down on Highgrade. His head vaporized under the double-barreled blast of Highgrade's shotgun. The horse fell, throwing the headless body before struggling to its feet and running away.

Windborne sparks, clouds of embers, were blown into the treetops. The top branches were heavy with snow, but dry underneath, and sticky with resin that flared up like oil.

Slocum stood atop the barrels in the wagon, firing above the heads of the panicked masses. Highgrade shucked empty shells from the shotgun, feeding it fresh ones. Other pockets of resistance were developing, but they were too diffuse to offer any really effective counter. Lines of light that were muzzle flares stabbed out from dark corners where groups of miners made a stand and fought back. But the darkness itself was fleeing, chased away by ever-mounting firelight. Now the trees were burning, too.

Outlaws roped the ridge poles of some of the smaller wood-en frame buildings and pulled them down atop those who sheltered inside. Larger structures, immune to such treatment, were put to the torch, their occupants shot down as they tried to escape.

Highgrade said, "This ain't a fight, it's a massacree!"

"Shut up and keep shooting," Slocum said.

A frightened running man tripped over one of the torch poles, knocking it into the wagon. The flaming torch barely touched one of the barrels before Slocum kicked it away, but it was enough. A small but significant amount of alcohol had leaked, droplets of whiskey having been sweated out of the joints between the staves. Its high-proof alcoholic content made it extremely inflammable.

Where the torch had grazed the side of the barrel, a little blue flame now glowed. With a *whoomp!* like the sound of a match being dropped in a pool of oil, the ring of flame expanded outward, overrunning the cask from top to bottom. An eerie, flickering blue aura, like the flame of a spirit lamp, or phosphorescent St. Elmo's fire.

Slocum reached for a blanket to smother it out, but before his hand closed on it, the flames reached the wagon bed, sticky with a quantity of spilled fluid. It flared up not blue, but with a bright hot yellow light, swiftly spreading from one end of the wagon to the other. This in turn ignited circles of blue flame at the base of all the barrels, which were swiftly enhaloed with their own flickering auras from bottom to top.

A blast sounded so close to Slocum that he was temporarily deafened in one ear. He had no cause for complaint, though, not when it was the roar of Highgrade's shotgun cutting down an outlaw who had ridden up on him from behind while he was transfixed by the growing blaze.

"Thanks!" he shouted.

Slocum's feet were warm. He looked down. Wisps of smoke from the burning barrel curled out from under the edges of his boot soles. The barrel shook from the liquid bubbling and boiling inside it. All of them did.

Slocum jumped down, stamping his feet in the snow to cool them. Ominous gurglings and spittings sounded from the blue-burning barrels. He went around to the back of the wagon, lowering the tailgate in hopes of saving some of his stores. The nearest barrels were swathed in blue flames, stopping him from laying hands on them.

A muffled explosion went *crump* inside a barrel. Nothing else happened for an instant, except that Highgrade took off running in the opposite direction. That decided Slocum. If Highgrade was abandoning ship, the cargo was well and truly lost.

He took off after Highgrade, overtaking him just as the next blast came. That was a real blast, a hellbender. Exploded by expanding gases, the barrel delivered its contents to naked flames, igniting a real conflagration. Flames leapt up fifty feet into the air, lighting up the night. The heat of it was intense against Slocum's back.

Highgrade stumbled and would have fallen had not Slocum grabbed him by the arm and held him upright until he recovered his balance. They kept running, blast after blast detonating behind them as one by one of the barrels became booming firebombs.

They staggered into a small hollow, huddling breathless while the whiskey wagon erupted like a volcano, belching heat and light, spewing tentacles of fire in all directions.

Highgrade spoke first, delivering what had to be the last word on Slocum's now-defunct entrepreneurial scheme.

"Hard come, easy go," he said.

"I'll kill 'em," Slocum said. "I'll kill 'em and piss on their corpses!"

"You don't have to shout, I'm right next to you."

"Sorry, I don't hear so good in one ear. By the way, thanks for nailing that varmint."

Highgrade shrugged. "Does this mean I don't get paid?"

"Can't hear you."

"I said, does this mean I don't get paid?!"

"I heard you the first time," Slocum said. "Don't worry about your dollars. I'll pay you out of the bounty I collect on their worthless hides."

"If they're worthless, how you gonna collect on them?"

Slocum didn't bother to answer, he was too busy reloading. "Lucky I keep plenty of rifle shells mixed in with the ammo on my gunbelt!"

Rifle rounds alternated with gun bullets in his belt loops, a strategy he had adopted long ago to prevent being caught short on just such an occasion. Everything else he owned had gone up with the wagon, and his horse was lost in the confusion.

It was good thing that he had paused to reload, for while he was doing so, fresh reinforcements arrived in the form of Blackie Hawkins and his Californians, who emerged from Hollander's Chute galloping toward the scene.

"Lord Almighty, there's more of them! What do we do now, Slocum?"

"Run!"

14

Tollin Proctor said, "What happened here, Hutty?"

"I figured you'd be cold from your long ride, so I lit a fire for you to warm up by."

"You figured right." Proctor chuckled, savoring the burning.

"Looks like you beat my boys to the punch," Hawkins said. "I like a man with initiative."

The turn of events had come as a surprise to Proctor, too, but he did his best to hide it and take the credit.

Heaps of embers and live coals overspread the ground, glowing like the lights of a distant city seen from a mountaintop. Great palls of smoke slanted across the valley, so thick that they resisted for a time the effort of the winds to blow them apart. The snowfall was thinning, turning to freezing rain.

Rumpus pointed toward the basin below the falls at the north of the cirque. "A bunch of them are forted up on the shelf by the lake."

"How many?"

"About fifty, boss, but it looks like there's no more'n ten, fifteen guns between them. We've been saving them for last. They ain't going nowhere. They're pinned with their backs to the wall."

Many had survived the massacre, fleeing in all directions, scattered, demoralized, beaten. They sought only to escape with their lives. The only pocket of resistance was on the shelf by the basin.

Proctor said, "It's your call, Hawkins."

"We finish them off now," Hawkins said.

"It'll be easy," Hutty said. "The slope's so low we can ride right up it. One charge, and we can sweep them clear off the shelf."

"What are we waiting for?" Hawkins said.

He had twelve men, counting himself. Proctor, his two side-men, and the rest of his gang numbered sixteen. Twenty-eight men in all, each one a deadly killer. They formed up into a group and rode toward the basin.

Come sunup, Hawkins would be in complete control of the valley and its priceless gold fields. He and Proctor and all their followers would file claims on the choicest sites, sewing them up, and establishing a clear and legal title to them. The way would be open for his masters in the San Francisco big-money combine to commence full-scale mining operations in the Kettle, free of the necessity of coming to terms with a crazy-quilt patchwork of stubborn, independent-minded claim holders. Monopoly is good business, the economic equivalent of a stacked deck.

Hoofs kicked up plumes of snow as the outlaws thundered into the draw leading to the Long Falls basin.

"Here they come!"

Moira Connell couldn't evict the fugitives sheltering on her land. She would have if she could, but there were too many of them for Julian Roux to roust, even with Dmitri backing him up. Besides, they had guns, too. Not many of them, but enough to turn the shelf into a killing field if gunplay developed. Already faced with death at the hands of the outlaws, they had nothing to lose by fighting to stay put.

There were about four score of them, mostly men, with some women and a few kids. Less than half had guns, handguns, with too few rifles and shotguns. They huddled behind what scant cover was available on the wide ledge, preparing for the imminent attack. Moira's group was apart from the rest, as far apart as they could be while still staying on the ledge. They had to stay, since there was no way out but the one that led straight into the oncoming horsemen.

Slocum and Highgrade squatted behind a big rock. Slocum fired up a cigar, puffing until its end glowed like a hot coal.

Highgrade said, "How about a smoke?"

"I'll save you some at the end."

"Better make it fast, because it looks like the end'll be pretty soon—what in tarnation are you grinning about, Slocum?"

Slocum reached into his inside coat pocket and took out a bundle of dynamite. "This time the blasting caps are in place."

"Glory be! What're you waiting for? Blast the varmints!"

"I've got a better idea. I'm going to give 'em a bath."

"Huh?"

"What do you think will happen when I blow a hole in the basin wall and let all the water out?"

Not waiting for a reply, Slocum rose, cigar chomped in the corner of his mouth as he scrambled across the ledge toward the basin, rifle in one hand, dynamite in the other.

After a pause, Highgrade trotted after him. "I'll cover you!"

Their path took them past the covert shielding Moira and company. Moira guessed the plan as soon as she saw the dynamite.

She said, "Stop them!"

"You crazy?" Julian said.

"It's my water and it's worth a fortune!"

"Not if you're dead."

"If you won't do something to stop them, I will!"

The basin's retaining wall was the product of a long-ago rockfall. Slocum and Highgrade scrambled across the cyclopean blocks at its lip, edging toward the V-shaped notch of the slipway.

Moira screamed, "STOP!"

That caught the attention of Slocum and Highgrade, and the sawed-off shotgun that Dmitri held leveled on them kept it.

Moira stood behind him. "Throw that dynamite in the lake!"

"I don't think so, lady," Slocum said.

"Do it or you'll die!"

"If I do, we'll all die—you included."

Pounding hoofs echoed up the draw like rolling thunder.

"They're coming fast," Slocum said.

"Dmitri, if he doesn't do what I said, kill him!"

Stray winds brought the scent of burning woodsmoke to Julian, unleashing a flood of memories.

"Mud flats," he said to himself.

There had been burning on the last job he had gone on with Blackie Hawkins and the gang back in San Francisco. A horde of squatters had built a shantytown on a stretch of tidal flats on the waterfront coveted by a steamship company that wanted to build a ferry terminal in the spot. Blackie had burned them out. The rickety tarpaper shacks had gone up faster than expected, trapping many of the squatters in the blaze. Men, women, and children burned to death in the holocaust . . .

Before he knew what was happening, a gun was in his hand, pointing at Moira and Dmitri.

"Lower your gun or I'll kill you, Dmitri," he said.

Dmitri didn't flinch, didn't move a muscle. Twin bores of the sawed-off shotgun remained locked on Slocum and Highgrade.

Moira was outraged. "Have you lost your mind? You're working for me, Julian!"

"I just quit."

"You dirty son of a—"

"Better make up your minds," Slocum said. "Time's a-wasting!"

A sledgehammer blow struck Julian from behind, accompanied by a deafening roar. He knew without looking that he'd been shot in the back by Belinda Gale. He'd forgotten about her. Staggered, he kept his footing, fighting to stay alive for just a few seconds more.

He shot Dmitri, emptying the revolver into his hulking form, jerking the trigger until it clicked on empty chambers. Moira stood there openmouthed. Dmitri just stood there, reeling, not falling.

Belinda Gale put two more shots into Julian's back. Lurching forward on tiptoes, he let the empty gun drop from his hand. Still coming, he twisted his wrist, tripping the spring catch that sent the four-barreled derringer hidden up his sleeve into his palm. Bringing it up, he shot Dmitri in the face, felling him. Dmitri toppled sideways, falling down the front of the basin wall.

Belinda Gale was so unnerved that her next shot barely tagged Julian's arm and the ones after that missed entirely.

Moira started to plead for her life, thought better of it, and spat in Julian's direction. Acknowledging the pleasantry with an ironic little head bow, he shot her in the chest—she was too beautiful to shoot in the head. She stretched her length across the rocks.

Julian fell facedown, swallowed up by the Great Dark before he hit the ground.

As if powered by some occult half-life of its own, Highgrade's shotgun roared, cutting down Belinda Gale. He stared bemusedly at the weapon in his hands. It was easier than looking at the mess it had made of the woman.

Slocum leapt into action, clambering down the rocks to the left of the spillway, wedging the bundle of dynamite securely in place in a crevice about a third of the way from the base of the wall. Touching the hot end of the cigar to the fuse, he lit it and clambered back up to the wall.

The head of the wedge of mounted outlaws wheeled into view, swinging around the last bend of the draw. In the vanguard were Blackie Hawkins, Tollin Proctor, Hutty, and Rumpus, closely trailed by two score more kindred damned souls. A fusillade burst from their guns as they charged. Slocum and Highgrade leapt to safety, diving flat on the ledge as the bullets smeared lead on the rock face overhead.

The bomb blew. Short fuse.

The blast obliterated those in the fore of the charge, mingling their atoms with tons of instantaneously pulverized rock. Where those rocks had been, nothing now existed to restrain the lakeful of cold black water that spewed into the draw, an irresistible juggernaut. Horses and men were mere straws in the foaming black torrent that whirled them to instant and utter destruction.

15

Highgrade wandered off in the early predawn hour. He'd spent a sleepless night mourning the tragic loss of the whiskey wagon. As the sky lightened, he felt the urge to be by himself, especially after having spent a long miserable night sharing the ledge with fifty other survivors. In that time, the snow had turned to rain and been washed away. The rain stopped; the sky cleared. It was colorless and cloudless when Highgrade set off on his walk. He didn't tell Slocum where he was going. He'd had enough of Slocum in the last few days. On the other hand, he didn't intend to go too far from the lanky gunman, either.

"He owes me money," Highgrade said to himself. He felt good about the debt. It gave him a moral leg up on Slocum. Slocum would somehow make good, of that he had no doubt. The man's own pride and sense of self was better surety of payment than any IOU.

"He sure talked some shit, now he's got to deliver," Highgrade said. "Just because he lost his shirt, why should I suffer? He won't be flat busted for long. Anybody who can shoot like that will never go hungry."

It wasn't hunger but thirst that tormented Highgrade. His mouth watered at the thought of all those barrels of redeye that had survived so many misadventures on the trail, only to suffer the fate of serving as fuel for a damned expensive bonfire. Thinking about the loss only made it worse. Not thinking about it was just as bad.

Through his gloom he dimly registered impressions of a vastly changed landscape. The basin had drained through the big break in the wall. Shallow pools dotted the black mud covering its now-exposed floor. The mud stank. The stream that had poured from the spillway was reduced to a thin trickle worming its way down the middle of the draw. Water still splashed down from the falls, but it would take a long, long time for it to fill the basin.

The torrent that had scoured the draw clean had spilled out a half mile on to the flat, turning a good part of the north valley into a soggy bog. In the distance, twisted corpses of drowned horses and outlaws lay scattered across the landscape, deposited where the flood had finally washed them up. Beyond, fingers of smoke rose from the charred sodden remains of the cremated town.

Movement atop a rise on the east bank of the draw caught Highgrade's eye. A small knot of cavorting figures—were they *dancing*? So it seemed, though they were too far away to tell. Highgrade ambled toward them for a better look.

Descending the slope from the ledge, he went south along the draw. The ground was wet, slick. He stepped carefully. The once swift-rushing stream was thinned out to a trickle no wider than a thin man's arm. The draw bore the marks of the violent flood that had swept through it due to the dynamiting of the basin wall. In that initial rush, boulders had been flung from the streambed and washed down to the flat; trees had been uprooted and ground into splinters; whole strata of the rock walls had been worn away.

Highgrade hadn't gone far when he remembered that he had left the shotgun back on the ledge. He started to go back for it, then changed his mind and continued onward. He wasn't going far. What could happen to him during this short walk? The outlaws had been smashed, and the six-gun stuck in the top of his pants would protect him against the unexpected. He resolved that he would never actually be out of sight of the ledge.

As he neared his destination, he slowed, staring in amazement. His eyes had not deceived him. He had indeed seen three figures gamboling in a clearing atop the east limb of the draw.

It was the pinheads he had discovered yesterday chained

in the back of Soapy Spellman's wagon. Somehow they had gotten free and escaped their keepers. Holding hands, they circled in a tireless variant of ring-around-the-rosie, innocent ecstatic faces upturned to the growing brightness in the sky that heralded the dawn.

"Well, if that don't beat all," Highgrade said. "They say the Lord looks after fools and drunkards, though."

Glinting brightness in the foreground drew his attention away from the pinheads to his immediate surroundings. Points of light sparkled in a crevice in the embankment. Reflected sunlight, no doubt. But the sun had not yet risen high enough to shine into this sheltered nook.

Highgrade blinked, rubbed his eyes. The brightness refused to go away. Frowning, eyes narrowed, he started toward it.

The flash flood had done what it would have taken a gang of pick-and-shovel men a month to do, clearing away tons of rocks and dirt within the space of a few moments. The hydraulic excavation had radically changed the contours of the draw, undercutting the banks, bringing to light that which had been buried for hundreds, perhaps thousands of years.

A sparkly mass of crystals lay sheltered in a rockbound cleft. Highgrade examined it wonderingly. The flood had unearthed a pocket of quartz known as "float," its cubed surfaces shot through with ropy strands of red-yellow color.

Highgrade shivered, weak-kneed. His heart beat so fast that he was afraid it was going to burst. He put his hand on his left breast to still the pounding. Dizziness seized him, vertigo.

"Can it be . . . ?" he whispered.

It could. It was. There could be no doubt. In his earlier days, before he'd turned drunk, he'd forgotten more about mining than most men would ever know, and the remnants of that expertise assured him in the rightness of his appraisal of the float rock.

Gold.

It was gold. The flood had uncovered a pocket of gold and he'd been the first to find it. Real gold, not fool's gold. He knew the difference. The color promised that the ore would assay out into big money. The surface deposit alone would be worth thousands of dollars, and who knew how deep the vein extended into the earth.

Highgrade sank to his knees, overcome by emotion. He didn't know whether to laugh or cry or do both, so he did neither.

He said, "I'm rich—rich!"

"No, you ain't," a voice said.

A rabbit who freezes when the shadow of a hawk overflies it experiences much the same sensation that now seized Highgrade. The blood in his veins turned to ice; his heart, to stone.

"Turn around and keep them hands where I can see them," the voice said.

Highgrade obeyed. Standing in the draw behind him was Rufe, a gun in his hand.

"You!" Highgrade said.

Rufe grinned, showing buck teeth. "Yeah, me. I was hiding up on the ridge when I saw you poking around down in the rocks. Figured I ought to take a looksee. Glad I did. I always wanted to be rich. Funny how things work out. I'm rich, and you—you're dead."

"Empty that gun into me, sonny boy, and I'll still last long enough to wring your neck like a chicken."

"You talk big," Rufe said. "Let's see how full of fight you are with a bullet in the guts, rumpot."

Rufe had just finished thumbing back the hammer when the top of his head exploded, killing him so fast that he didn't even have time to be surprised that he was dead.

Slocum stepped into view from behind some bushes where he'd been hiding, smoke rising from the muzzle of his Winchester. His clear-eyed gaze took in the whole scene: Rufe's corpse, Highgrade, and the gold. He grinned.

"Howdy, partner," said Slocum.

A special offer for people who enjoy reading the best Westerns published today.

WESTERNS!

NO OBLIGATION

Mail the coupon below

To start your subscription and receive 2 FREE WESTERNS, fill out the coupon below and mail it today. We'll send your first shipment which includes 2 FREE BOOKS as soon as we receive it.